JON HILLMAN

THE CRYSTAL KEEP

LENNAN

The crusted snow of the forest floor cracked beneath Lennan's feet as he traipsed between the fallen branches and last remnants of autumnal undergrowth. Once tightly-packed fir trees gently began to part as the forest edge drew closer, ushering strips of cold blue sky and deep grey landscapes into view. At last, Lennan found himself stood at the boundary of the dense woodland, the perfect natural barrier to a town encased. That had been some trek, and now there she was in full view, Mt. Spitertind. Some mountain. Some beauty. And she would be some home, too. Lennan was joined on the treeline by companions Cecil and Cecil's young son, Russel. The men and the boy of the Crystal Order drank of the chilled winter air and exhaled in exultation. The sharp peak of the solo mountain soared high into the skies, tickling the underbellies of thin clouds above. The snow blanket over her summit draped more than halfway down to her base, and at those rocky and tree-spattered roots a sizeable town had settled. Elsdale, just as reported by the initial scouts, nestled within the shadows of the south face of the mountain: the only civilisation to be found around it. Even at this distance, the sounds of busy townsfolk and laughing children could be heard on the light breeze. Livestock bleating and clucking, tools chopping wood and breaking earth.

"Scout's'll be right about this one, for once, I reckon," Cecil said in his usual gruff tones as he leaned in to Lennan.

The sound of Cecil rubbing his bristled chin in thought had Lennan considering whether the man wore a beard or a mask of iron filings. He had made less noise pushing through the low branches of the forest. "Oh, they will indeed," he replied, ending his scrutiny of Cecil's chin, "and the scout is still there, posing as an innkeeper with his son. Good man. He wouldn't have remained in the area if he hadn't believed. Few mountains are as grand as this one, my friend. Perhaps it is not the first time she has played host to a fledgling?"

"Perhaps not."

"Is it really far to the top?" young Russel piped up. Hints of despair fluttered in his words.

"Son," Cecil grunted, "the height of Spitertind is not the journey we are concerned with. We are here to embark on a journey of birth and life, and we-"

"I know, I know, I-"

Cecil clipped the side Russel's ear with his gauntleted hand. A crow screeched from a branch above and took off. Flecks of snow fell down between the feet of the group. Lennan watched the crow fly over Elsdale, not wanting to look at either Cecil or the boy.

"Don't interrupt me, boy. Don't seem to realise how lucky you are to be assigned here. Most men of our Order miss the laying or the birthing. You're young enough to witness the entire cycle. You may even live long enough to be involved with another."

"Yes, father."

Lennan bit his tongue. The birthing was a long process, and a man's life was short. Still, he wasn't so stupid as to interrupt a lesson from father to son. Lennan had seen thirty-two winters himself and had been starting to worry that he would be one of those wasted lives that Cecil referred to; one that only saw the beginning and not the end, or worse, nothing at all. It would put him in line with many members of the Order, but Lennan had always felt that there was more in store for him than mere disappointment. Something grander. He knew that he was more important than the general rabble that joined the Order. His family, his title, his education all spoke of this. What he needed was the event. This magnificent mountain was the proof that he was destined for more. Spitertind was a gift. He could hold on until the end, he could see the whole cycle through; the Order were becoming rather good at speeding along the process now. Whether or not Cecil could make it was another matter. The swordsman had another ten years on Lennan, though the gruff bastard was as determined and devout a man as Lennan had ever met. And yet, despite Cecil's devotion to the cause of the Crystal Order, he had remained a man of action and exploration. The swordsman was more than capable of taking on the mantle of priesthood, but apparently that side of things just didn't appeal to him. Fortunate for Lennan that he didn't have a rival with him. Cecil was a fine man to have at one's side in the shadow of danger, and he was going to become pivotal in dealing with the folk that called the base of Mt. Spitertind their home. Oh, there would be trouble once these simple men, women, and children realised their destinies. There always was. "Shall we pay this Elsdale a visit, then?" Lennan spoke without facing either of his companions. "Not an old town, but one with a decent enough population and wholly self-sufficient with it; not many ties to the outside. Ideal for our needs. Once we're settled in, we'll call in the others and position scouts in these forests; they're going to prove very useful in making sure the good people of Elsdale stay where we need them."

"Aye, they will," Cecil agreed. "But before any of that, we do need to confirm that Spitertind really *is* the place. We need the full lay of the land, the secrets, the local knowledge. I don't doubt the scouts, but they've been wrong before. Place feels right, but I need to see it all with my own eyes first. What say we stay the night in the town, fill our bellies, and set out at first light tomorrow?"

"Of course, of course, my friend. We've travelled a long way. A rest for our chilled bones will do us all a favour. Now, Russel," Lennan knelt in the snow to put himself at eye-level with the boy. His thin trousers soaked through to the knees immediately. "Do your father and I a favour and run along into the town. Take this." Lennan thrust a small pouch filled with coins into the lad's hands. "Find the inn owned by a large man and his fat little son, the lad'll be about your age, if I'm not mistaken. I have it on good authority that the other inn in town is under the ownership of a young lady. Leave that one be for now, and when you do find the right one see to it that we have a room to ourselves, do you hear? Your father and I will have much to discuss this evening, and we'd rather the details stay between ourselves."

Russel's red cheeks swelled with a smile. The boy snatched the purse, nodded, and ran off across the frosty grass towards the town.

"He's a good lad," Lennan said.

Cecil grunted, then sniffed. "He's got a lot ahead of him, and he misses his mother too much." He fingered a ring on a chain about his neck.

"That'll all be forgotten once he comes face to face with our Lord, Cecil, and you know it. There is no sight quite so grand in all of Traverne, and your son will soon see that. We'll all soon see that."

"Right you are," Cecil agreed. "Their visage is grand, indeed. *If* it is here."

Lennan tried not to let frustration reach his eyes and lips. This wasn't the time for silly arguments. Cecil had met a Lord before. Even if he hadn't been present for the whole cycle, he had been there for some of it and that was more than Lennan could say. He strode ahead, taking his first steps towards the town. Russel had already reached the closest of the log cabins and was no more than a small, bounding shape in the distance. Lennan found himself staring at Mt. Spitertind in awe. All of the disappointment that had come before was nothing now. All had been leading up to this.

This was the place.

Chapter One

LOST FOR WORDS

"No, Haggar, no you really bloody can't," Marigold groaned as he eyeballed his confused friend. Tears of mirth streamed from his eyes, over his cheeks, and into his braided beard. A few drops managed to escape and tapped onto the greasy wood of the bar beneath his elbows. "By Greldin, man, you cannot breathe fire!"

"I fucking can! Did it last night with Lisbeth's brew. Strong stuff. Shitting strong stuff. It'll burn you a new arsehole if you down too much of it. And that's where it got me thinking, how about I burn something else? Yeah, I might have been on my own, out of sight, but that don't mean I didn't manage it! I fucking did it, Chief! I did! I'm serious. Deadly fucking serious!"

Chief. The mere mention of the title still had Marigold looking to his side for Torsten. It hadn't quite sunk in that it was for him now. An axe buried in the late Torsten's skull had ended his reign as clan Chief only a few weeks ago. Prematurely, even by barbarian standards. Yet, even on that day, before the dead Chief's blood had soaked into the earth and the circling crows descended for the eyes and tongue, the surviving clan had already begun looking to Marigold for new orders. Fair enough, they had all been in the middle of a scrap and somebody needed to direct it; Marigold was the strongest, the loudest, and usually the one with the ideas. It had to have been dumb luck that nobody had since contested the decision after blades were cleaned and arrows plucked. Nevertheless, Marigold didn't feel like a Chief. Torsten had had to fight for his life on more than one occasion on the very same day as picking up the title. What did Marigold get? Weeks of nothing, and now Haggar trying to impress him with a useless skill, no doubt learned simply for the wowing of impressionable young women. Torsten never had to deal with this kind of shit, but perhaps that was simply down to him searching for his next fight before the current one ended. A good but violent man, Torsten.

Haggar was rapidly tapping at Marigold's shoulders. Memories of Torsten's face disappeared like smoke into the air. Haggar had always been a man for grand claims, and now that his oldest friend had become his superior, it seemed that he wanted to impress him more than ever. The problem here was that breathing fire wasn't really doing it for Marigold. If he had come to him with rukh wrestling claims, he might have been happier about it – those great, shaggy birds would put on a show even if Haggar couldn't – but, that wasn't the offer. Fire was.

"Alright, alright, Haggar, whatever you say." Marigold waved a hand in Haggar's face and swung around on his stool, returning to the bar. His chest still ached from the spasms of laughter, before mirth had become annoyance. As he ran his fingers along old grooves etched into the bar from the years of cups and cutlery hitting it, he cast a sideways glance at Magnus. His bald head lay nestled within in his massive arms on the counter. Too much drink? Doubtful: Marigold hadn't clocked him with any more than he'd had himself. Simple embarrassment was more likely. Took a lot to embarrass a barbarian. Almost as much as it took to get one pissed. Beyond the giant, Marigold's other companion sat braying, trying to stand out. Young Pettar, surrounded with several empty cups. Probably just for show, probably only arranged that way to prove that he was just as immune to the effects of ale as any other barbarian; Marigold hadn't actually seen him emptying a single one. Nevertheless, the young lad – still in his teen years – was slapping the bar with an open palm in time with his uneven guffawing. His long and pale brown hair was wild, unbraided. Greasy from hands that kept sliding it aside. He certainly sounded inebriated. Evidently, Marigold wasn't the only one that doubted their fire-loving friend's claims.

"What? Hey, no! No! Don't be like that, Mari!" Haggar grabbed his Chief's shoulders again and spun him back around. The smoky room blurred as Marigold's dirty-yellow braid of hair slapped him across the face. "How long've you known me? When last the time was I midn't danage to do… to do something I said I said… I said I would? If the half-brained Gillfolk can do it, why the fuck don't you believe I can?"

"Man, have you heard yourself?" Marigold shook Haggar. "How much have you had? I don't know about fire, but you're spewing a lot of hot piss. Also, the half-brained Gillfolk breathe swamp fumes and eat rotten flesh. The gassy little fuckers are infernos waiting to happen, why the fuck do you think they hate Sear so much?" Marigold growled, deliberately removing Haggar's hands from his shoulders. They hung lifelessly at his drunk friend's sides. "There was a time I thought *you* had more than half a brain. I'm not so bloody sure about that now." The man was barely any younger than he was, and after forty-odd winters, such idiotic ideas had long since left Marigold's thoughts. Haggar ought to be past this idiocy by now. Pettar, perhaps, but Haggar? This is what happened to a man when he didn't have a woman. The child never left. "Maybe you should have another cup, maybe that'll finish you off and put this Pits-forsaken idea out of your head. We're here to meet the folk, not burn them all down." More than a few worried faces perked up at *that* suggestion.

"Look," Haggar leaned in close, eyes rolling in his head as a string of thick drool leaked down his chin. He began to whisper, barely audible above the hum of the inn and the rhythmic 'thunk' of darts hitting a board on the wall, "just look at those girls over there." He licked the spit from his chin and jerked his shadowed head in the direction of a table in the corner of the inn. A table surrounded by women, or girls on the cusp of womanhood. "Look at them!" he cried, jabbing the air behind them. It was about as inconspicuous as a drunken warrior could be. "They've had their eyes on me all night."

"Probably making sure you're not coming over!"

"Well, yeah, er, no! But look, four of them! All eyes on me."

"Every eye in this pissing building is on you at the moment, Hag. Perhaps they're scared of the big bastard watching them? Or maybe they want to see what damage you'll do to yourself when you trip over your own stool and headbutt the counter? You give any of that a second thought? I don't think any of the locals are particularly pleased to see us here, so let's not make them right, eh?" The girls *were* an eyeful now that Marigold glanced them over. Too young for men. Not at all suited to a barbarian. They ought to be wandering the woods with lads their own age. They also looked markedly worried. "Anyway, they're not looking at you now."

"No, of course they're not. You just gone and told the damn room I can't breathe fire and that I'm a halfwit."

Marigold blinked. "I'm fairly sure they didn't hear that, Haggar, but they were statements of fact, regardless."

"Marigold." Haggar licked his lips and closed his eyes, steadying himself. "Marigold, I can bloody do it, I can. I will. And they'll be flies on *fucking* rukh shit for it, I'm telling ya."

"Greldin wept... well-" Marigold bit his tongue and looked around the room. The night at this inn had been rather quiet, if you took away all the murmurings from folk expecting a slaughter at any moment. Decent place, but perhaps it *could* do with a little livening up. Let the locals know what Marigold and his men were really about. Well, not breathing fire, but worth a bit of entertainment, at least. All he had wanted from this evening was to get to know the place, see the kind of folk he might be rubbing shoulders with on a more regular basis. Maybe this little stunt would answer whether or not that would actually be possible. "You *really* want to be the rukh shit, Haggar?"

Haggar nodded like a happy dog.

Marigold slammed his fist down on the bar, knuckles white and tight. Horns and cups along the smooth, shiny platform bounced with the blow. Two of Pettar's fell over, spilling dregs over the wood. "Barkeep! What's the strongest liquor you've got behind there, eh? Come on, let's have it out." He struck the counter again for good measure. The general hubbub hushed.

The barkeep, a short and tubby man with a black mop of hair that he'd let fall over his eyes, had been quivering within the gloomy depths behind the counter ever since Marigold and his friends had refused his suggestion of finding somewhere else to drink that evening, somewhere away from the settlement. He smiled faintly, maintaining an uneasy look of trepidation that folk always reserved for dealings with men bigger than themselves. He nodded quickly, and within a heartbeat had disappeared from sight below the bar. Bottles and jars clinked and clashed as the man rummaged furiously. Marigold peered over, vaguely expecting the man to produce a stashed bow or other ranged weapon. *That* would be a bit of fun. A hand emerged instead, clutching at a half-empty bottle with a thick, brown liquid that frothed as it danced. The Chief was a little disappointed. The glass was clear, though filthy. The rest of the man joined the hand and bottle. The wary barkeep's arm reached gingerly outwards, keeping the bottle as far from himself as possible. He mumbled, though he avoided eye contact, "...'ll put hairs on your chest, that will."

"Good. Pay the man, Magnus," Marigold barked as he snatched the drink from the proprietor's hand. Marigold didn't have a clue what cost what out here in the 'civilised' world. The concept of coin was ridiculous. Why trade something flat, metal, and useless, when you could simply swap for something the other needs? Who decided the value? The one getting the money always wanted more, regardless of what he was exchanging. Demands went up but the items gained back always remained the same quality and amount. Marigold didn't have time for the stuff at all. Despite this, all the folk in the villages, towns, and cities everywhere else he had travelled seemed to love the stuff, and Magnus was keen on keeping a coin or two to himself. Perhaps Marigold was the one that was out of touch, as unlikely as that seemed.

Magnus flicked a matte grey disc with a hole in the middle over the bar and into the owner's stained apron. "That do ya, fella?" he shouted over the din. The poor man failed to grapple the coin and began fumbling around behind the counter for it. He returned after a moment twirling the coin in his fingers and nodding in acceptance. Sweat beaded the balding forehead that had been revealed in his panic. "Pretty reasonable, Boss, if he lets us have the lot for it." The proprietor's face dropped.

"Doubt he'll argue about it," Marigold said, staring the man out. "Right," he bellowed, "Ladies and gentlemen." He spun around on his stool to address the folk of the tavern, "...and children." If anyone was going to enjoy this show it would be the younger ones. His cheeks twitched involuntarily as he watched men and women and kids put down their drinks and cutlery. His eyebrows raised as a gnarled, skinny man threw his last dart before realising he was the one they were waiting for. The red-cheeked man shuffled back into the crowd. "This prick," Marigold continued, gesturing at Haggar, "is going to show us how to breathe fire. A bit of entertainment for us all, whatever the result of it might be." Marigold watched Haggar grinning, trying his hardest to look around the whole room but failing miserably in tearing his eyes from the table of young women he was so blatantly interested in. Greldin's teeth, they were all bloody-well smirking back, fluttering their eyes and lapping up his muscles. Perhaps old Hag wasn't completely mad after all. Marigold ran an ale-soaked finger beneath the fur cloak around his neck. It was hot enough in this inn already without adding flames to the mix, but there they were. "Keep your drinks close by," he said, pointing at each and every one of the crowd, "the fool'll need dousing in a moment." Marigold twisted to locate the scratching that was building behind him. There was the poor barkeep, forcing himself as far into a corner as possible. Fuck's sake, the blaze was going to be headed the other way. Marigold mouthed some words of reassurance to the stricken man, though it didn't change his countenance. Shit. He hoped that Magnus had enough on him to pay for the inevitable damages. Fine way to ingratiate yourselves with the locals in a land you planned on settling. He returned to the crowd, a half-circle of them surrounded the star of the show, eager-eyed young ones crouched at the front. For a group that had shown marked distress at the arrival of Marigold and his men, they really had resolved those fears now that one of the barbarians was putting his life in danger. Bloodthirsty bastards, the lot of them. Everyone was, really. Human nature. Marigold shook his head gently as Haggar pulled his shirt over his braided head, baring his glistening chest to the room. And there were the whoops from the girls. Haggar knew what he was doing. He was a clever idiot. Marigold popped the cork from the bottle with a squeak and inhaled the fumes. It wasn't often that Marigold coughed at the scent of liquor, but this was one such occasion. This shit was strong enough to get pissed on from inhalation alone. He held the bottle out to Haggar.

"Chief." Haggar nodded solemnly, wrapping his fingers around the neck of the bottle. He formed an 'O' around the rim and chugged. His eyes widened considerably as he swilled the liquid about his mouth.

"Burning hot enough for you already, Haggar?" Marigold slapped his knee in delight as he watched. "Still want your fire?"

Haggar nodded vehemently, cheeks full.

"Let's have it, then." Marigold took the bottle and shirt from Haggar. He stuffed the fabric around the top and held it upside down to soak it. One of the excited village men squeezed to the front of the gathering with a flickering candle he had plucked from a fixture on the wall. "For the initiative, the honours are yours." Marigold pushed the bottle into the flame.

The fabric burst alight alright.

Haggar reached out blindly; more than a hint of desperation shook his fingers. Seems they had finally discovered a beverage that could best the man.

"Sure you're ready for this, Hag?" Marigold asked quietly.

Haggar's full cheeks quivered.

"You're a fucking idiot, you know that?"

Haggar's rapid nodding and full cheeks fired a spurt of alcohol from his pursed lips. The fire leapt from the bottle, eager for the additional fuel. Haggar squeezed and blew into the burning wick of twisted shirt. A jet of white-hot flame spread out through the room with a roar. Whoops and hollers rose as folk of all ages jerked back and patted singed hair.

"Fuck me, the man *can* breathe fire," cried Marigold.

"Again," cried the crowd as one.

Again, Haggar blew, scorching the low ceiling, adding more smoke to an already murky room. The bartender was hugging his sides, shaking his head. Apologies were going to have to come.

"Again," they demanded.

Haggar swallowed and breathed in heavily for the encore. That was the mistake. The one Marigold had always known was inevitable at some point this evening. Inside the flame rushed, settling deep within the showman's mouth. Haggar's eyes widened, his jaw trembled, his cheeks bloomed red. The stricken barbarian bellowed like a wounded bear, fingers scraping at his chin, his neck, his teeth. The bottle fell, shattering on the floorboards. Marigold leapt to stamping out the flames as Haggar crashed through the crowd, sending them careening over tables and chairs as he rushed to the exit. Cries of excitement fast became wails of terror as the frenzied barbarian stumbled over and through them. Hinges squealed as the door was flung open. Flakes of snow were exchanged for the topless, burning fool. Haggar was out.

"By Greldin, lads, didn't I tell him this was a stupid fucking idea?"

"You did, you did, Chief," Pettar said, wide-eyed and glaring at the door. "Shall I go see how he is?"

"Pit-cursed idiot," Marigold muttered. "Aye, Pettar, off you go. Show's over, everyone, back to your drinks."

Folk began to return from the edges of the room. Chairs scraped back into position as whispers grew into conversation and the hammering of darts started up again. Pettar set the door swinging himself as he left. The small fire was gone but circular scorches stained the floor and ceiling. There were also several tables and chairs resting in pieces in the line between the bar and the door. Marigold wasn't really one for apologies, but he offered the bartender – who had since dropped fear for silent outrage – the remaining coins from Magnus' pouch nevertheless. Only two of the girls remained at the table, whispering in hushed tones to one another while snatching glances at Marigold and Magnus. Perhaps the other two had gone to see how Haggar was. Perhaps the fool actually got what he had been after. Two out of four wasn't bad. It wasn't bad at all. Marigold shook his head and ordered himself and Magnus another cup. Lucky for them the barkeep didn't appear to have the stones to kick them out. Between sips, snatches of conversation told that tonight's incident would remain on local lips for a time to come.

The door creaked open again, and a set of footsteps tapped slowly across the floorboards. Too measured for a quick recovery from Haggar. No, these were heavy, booted feet, and they belonged to more than two men. Marigold kept his eyes on the bar. The room hushed to a low murmur as the feet approached the middle of the room. Six feet, three men, by Marigold's reckoning. One set of steps continued, coming to a stop by the bar. The man leaned forwards, resting on the counter by Marigold's side. The Chief glanced without moving his head. Rings decorated all but one of the fingers that gripped the wet and sticky wood. A yellowed, leather bracer covered a white sleeve, running up to a bright blue cloak that hung over the man's side.

"So, this is where you're all hiding again, is it?" the man said. The voice was harsh, dripping with disdain. "Well, whether you're pickled or not, our *Lord*" he noticeably lengthened the title, "still requires more of you. Any volunteers this time, or will I have to choose for myself once again?"

Feet from the patrons scuttled on the floor. Back they went.

"Choose?" Marigold asked with a tone of genuine interest. He turned on his stool to face the man. Not an unattractive fellow, Marigold noted, but the large, hooked nose was somewhat unfortunate. The newcomer's tousled black hair still had flakes of snow melting in it, and his cold, blue eyes shot contempt at each of the patrons. "Choose for what?" Marigold asked again.

"Ah," the man stared Marigold in the eyes, "a volunteer perhaps?"

"Not fucking likely, you're not my type."

The two men nearer the door – footmen perhaps and caped just like the cold man – pulled blades halfway from sheathes on their belts. The cold man raised an opened palm in their direction.

Marigold remained seated, calmly glancing at the men before returning his gaze to the fellow at the bar. "I'll ask again, friend. Choose them for what?" By Greldin, he wasn't going to be intimidated by some stoneless fuckwit out here in the middle of nowhere.

"Obviously you're not from around here, are you, mister...?"

"Marigold."

A stifled cry came from one of the children in the crowd. This man was clearly no friend of the town.

"Marigold." The man sniffed deeply and looked at the ceiling, noticing the scorch mark. He drummed his fingers on the bar. "Marigold, eh? I may have heard the name."

Marigold didn't like that tone. "Aye, you might have. I've killed a lot of cunts, and word of that tends to spread around to the other cunts I've not killed yet."

Chill, blue eyes met steely, grey eyes. The newcomer and Marigold glared at each other for a few uneasy seconds.

"Men!" the cold man barked.

In a heartbeat, Marigold whipped a dagger from his belt and pinned the bastard to the bar by his hand. His yell was doused by the rising cacophony of scraping tables and chairs and shrieks of panic as all patrons pressed against the walls. Magnus kicked his stool back and charged towards the two footmen in the middle of the inn. The men were armed but Magnus's fists were more than a match for the pair of them. Even with their steel, the closest of the two struggled to retrieve his blade from its icy sheath. He had a split-second to stare wide-eyed at Magnus before his jaw shattered beneath the first blow. Behind the counter, the barkeep's face drained in horror. Trembling arms reached out, then recoiled to his mouth, furiously chewing nails to the blood.

"Knife! He's got a knife!" a voice cried from within the tangle of townsfolk.

"Finish him! Finish it all now," barked the unnamed man, flailing with his free hand.

Marigold left the apparent leader fastened where he was and unceremoniously snapped the neck of the knife-wielding footman. The coward had been about to stab Magnus in the back. Meanwhile, Magnus himself was making fine work of reducing the other sap's face to a red mulch.

"I'll ask again," Marigold spoke into the room. "Choose them fo-" His demand was silenced by a savage blow to the back of his head. His time for the axe already? Stars danced in his eyes as he dropped to one knee, fuzz claiming his head. Splinters of wood fell around him. No axe, just a chair. The cold man barged Marigold aside, knocking him into Magnus.

"You!" the man hissed. "You're coming with me."

Marigold squinted to see the man viciously yanking the arm of one of the girls Haggar had been watching. She shrieked as he dragged her towards the door.

"Our Lord will have what he damn well wants! Fools, the lot of you. Always making this harder on yourselves. Everything could be so bloody simple, but no, you give me the run about every fucking time!"

Lord? Marigold knew of no Lord around here. Not in here, or Leandyke beyond the plains, or even Whitehall on the edges of Illis. There weren't even any major strongholds or towers that would hold a man of such a title. This prick was a loon. Marigold breathed in sharply and dragged himself up. At that moment, Haggar staggered back in through the door, bloodied mouth agape and bare chest glistening with melted snow. The burnt barbarian took one look at the cold man and then one at the young woman struggling behind him. A grimace that could crack glass contorted his face. Without any further hesitation, Haggar smashed his forehead directly into the fellow's nose. A cascade of red dashed Haggar as the blue cloaked man crumpled to the floor in a heap. Out cold. Pathetic. The girl shook herself free of the clinging hand and gave a prim snort, kicking the cold man in the ribs for good measure. Haggar grinned at her. He looked like something from the damn Pits with his blood mask and wild, white eyes. He dropped to one knee and slid his dagger between the man's ribs. The man didn't wake, nor would he again. The inn door swung open, admitting Pettar and a cloud of snow.

"Fuck me, Chief, you can't just have a quiet drink, can you?" Pettar surveyed the mess and whistled. "Three dead bastards." He appeared somewhat jealous; poor lad hadn't been in many fights.

Marigold raised his eyebrows and finally pushed himself up to standing, still rubbing the back of his head. He gave himself a once over and was disappointed to find a sizeable hole in his trousers over his left knee. He opened his mouth to speak, but a voice from behind beat him to it.

"You enormous bloody fools!" The owner of the establishment shrieked. "Damned, sodding barbarians. Death first, questions later. Don't give two shits who you kill, do you? Can you even begin to fathom the mess you've dragged me into? Us into? Can you? You, Marigold, was it? You've really done it now. We're doomed. They'll be back! They'll be back with more, and they won't give me… me or anybody else a choice to give themselves up next time, they'll take the fucking lot of us! Fyr save us. We could have lost one, now we're all for it."

The patrons that had been stunned into silence by the assault began to murmur and moan.

"He's right," hissed a hag. "Look what you've done."

"Aye, we don't want no trouble with you, but don't leave us with this mess," another voice slipped out.

"Fine work, I say," a proud woman in a red headscarf declared, stamping a booted foot on the ground as she threw a fork at the corpse. It clattered to the floor.

"You going to finish the rest of them off?" an old man demanded, shaking his frail fist into the air.

"Hey… w-what?" Marigold was puzzled. The trio were dead, nobody was telling anybody anything anytime soon. He expected a little more gratitude if he was being honest. "Look, if your Fyr was even half a god, you wouldn't have had these blue-cloaked pricks walking into your bar and choosing people in the first place; a proper god would have put an end to it already. I bet *this* was the first time anybody even said 'No' to the bastard. It was, wasn't it? Wasn't it?" He shouted. "How long's this been going on? Who are they? Where were they going to take her?" He gestured at the girl who was now sat comfortably on Haggar's knee by the door, busy running her fingers up and down his thick arms. Fucking typical.

"*They* are the *'Crystal Order'*, you ignorant brute," the proprietor began. "A cult. They've settled high up in the mountains behind us, on the peak of Spitertind, if we're to believe them. They serve some *Lord* or other, I don't know, they don't tell us anything more than that, just that this ruler needs more people, whoever he is, for it is 'His Will'. And that?" He pointed at the dead man as his voice burst up an octave. "That's Russel bleeding all over my sodding floor. I don't know who the other two were, but Russel was... w-was one of their high-ups. A-an important man." The fellow was scratching the flesh on his neck red raw. "They won't be happy when he doesn't return, be even less happy when they find out he's fucking dead!"

"Oh alright, calm down, you prick," Marigold dismissed. "Clearly this Russel needed killing, none of you are going to deny that, right? Right?" Marigold took a deep breath, which had the happy effect of silencing the inn entirely. "So, what's been happening in this tiny bloody town? You just been letting them come down here and take who they want? Hand folk over to men that openly claim to be part of some pissing cult?" Marigold asked, and with some incredulity too.

"Sometimes people volunteer."

"So, they just take who they want?"

"Well, yes."

"And what are the 'volunteering' for?"

"I don't know!"

"Then how long's it been going on?"

"It's been a while."

"How long, *exactly*?" Marigold walked up to the bar, staring down at the aproned man. He was almost twice as tall as the trembling owner.

"L-longer than I've been running this inn, I-I don't know how long. Since my father owned it, not before. He's gone. There used to be far more of us than there are now. Now we all fit in here, and we tend to stick to together in here, now that..."

"That what?"

"That Ellen has gone, the other proprietor. Safety in numbers, us all being together."

Marigold had no words. The bartender wasn't even young, perhaps approaching Marigold's age. Now that he thought back on it, there hadn't been many folk in the streets outside the bar, none hunting the woods, and few candles lit in any windows. If anything, it had been *eerily* quiet. There were a lot of houses and huts in the town, though they had noted that most seemed empty upon their arrival, or at least the windows were. Maybe they actually were all here. Perhaps this portly fellow was right, safety in numbers and all that. Less chance of being 'chosen' if you were huddled together in a group.

"What's your name, man? And who speaks for this town?" Magnus asked, getting up and smearing a stream of sweat from his hairless head. He shook the sweat and remaining blood from his fists and picked up a stool, setting it by the bar next to Marigold. He sat down, resting his arms on the counter and his chin on his arms. He smiled.

"Err, I'm... I'm Christian. And... and nobody speaks for us, or Elsdale, not anymore, alright? They took *him* two months ago."

"So how many've they taken, over these years that nobody can put a fucking number to?" Marigold demanded.

"It wasn't many at first, maybe one every other month, but this last year it's been getting worse, one a week, maybe more."

"For fuck's sake, why haven't you fought back, Christian?" asked Magnus, cracking his knuckles. "These pieces of rukh shit didn't put up much of a fight, all things considered. I've fought goats that gave me more trouble. Lots of you around, too. You could take them on if you were all in on it."

"Look at us," the barkeep insisted. "Woodcutters, farmers, tanners, seamstresses; we're not cut out to fight armed men."

"Even so, you seem to have grown some stones in the last few moments," Magnus chuckled, "yelling at the Chief like that. Why not put that rage to the cult?"

"Aye," said Marigold. "Looks like you speak for this place now, Christian, what was it? Elsdale?" Christian recoiled from the bar, turning whiter than the drifting snow outside. The night really wasn't going very well for him. "Right, so they're up in the mountain?" Marigold asked.

"Y-yes, right at the top, I believe. I've not been up there myself, but that's where they seem to come from."

"Lucky for you then, Christian, and the gathered people of Elsdale," Marigold glanced to his sides, "You're not going to have to worry about them much longer." He received a clap on the shoulder from Magnus.

"Y-y-you'd do that? For us?"

Chatter rose from the men and women by the walls. They were starting to filter back out to the tables, turning them back over, sitting down. Snippets of excitement, of questions, of worry... Of changes afoot.

"Do it? Yes, we'll do it. For you? No."

"I beg your pardon?" Christian said, wringing his hands.

"We've been looking for a space to settle, you see. Got groups to the south, the east. Me and my detachment took the north, saw that huge fucking mountain out there, surrounded by a shield of trees. Had to take a look, and here we are. The plains outside your little Elsdale, Illis, eh? Seems like a fine place but we don't want any nasty surprises waiting for us," Marigold said, nodding with reverence for the green fields and iron-rich hills he had passed in the preceding weeks. The clan had always been nomadic, and recently that had been a requirement with the bloodthirsty Torsten at the helm. Marigold's first decision as leader was to stay put, fix weapons, let children grow up somewhere they weren't going to be driven from or have to lose half the clan fighting for. Shit, the clan needed more children after all the lives lost in the last year. Out here on the plains there were few enemies that Marigold knew of. This cult seemed like the first and the last of them. Couldn't be a big cult, for he'd had neither sight nor sound of the bastards since his arrival in the area. A small outfit no doubt. An easy win. Them being so close to his chosen avenue of investigation was a gift, a first job, mission, quest. A nearby victory. He studied the patrons as he looked around the inn, noting a great deal of concern on faces now that his plans were out in the open. "Illis is big. Lots of space for us to spread out our yurts, let our rukhs run free, have our goats graze. We've been scouting it for some time, and we're about ready to settle. Rest of the clan is set a short ride from here investigating the other towns and villages. There aren't many, and that's just how we like it. Good woodland in Illis, good iron in the hills. No fucking wizards that I've been able to root out either." Indeed, there were just a handful of empty towers that somebody else must have cleared already. "But, we're going to have a hard time settling here if we've some Pit-forsaken fucking cult rushing down from the mountains to give us shit every other week. That, Christian, I just can't abide. We'll come to blows sooner or later, and I'd rather on a rukh. Nothing any of his men couldn't handle if he went awry, but some local knowledge would be a boon in a land Marigold had merely walked a straight line through. "Alright then. Join us, I don't know where we're going anyway. You can guide us to where we need to be, right?"

"Oh yes, right up, so we go."

"Just remember though, I don't expect you to get yourself into a mess that you can't get yourself out of. I don't want someone along that'll just slow us down, alright?"

"Of course, of course! That's fine by me, sir. I can handle m'self, so I can." He pulled the axe from a loop on his belt and twirled it.

"Very impressive. Could have used that earlier. And Marigold will do. I don't want any of this 'sir' shit where I'm concerned, and I don't want you calling me 'Chief', either."

"Very well, Marigold." Ramage offered his hand.

"Good to have you along," grinned Magnus, taking the hand before Marigold could. "Might even make a proper fighter out of yous." Magnus leaned over to Marigold. "Got us a nice little job, Chief! Enjoying bein' Chief, Chief?"

"Aye," Marigold deadpanned. "It's not a lot different from not being Chief, eh?"

Magnus barked a laugh and finished his drink with a slurp. He slammed the cup down.

The inn returned to normal operations. Darts, drinking, chattering. The bodies were left where they were, though. Folk in all corners eyed Marigold and his men, while Ramage stood awkwardly by their side. Marigold heard 'Ramage' and 'madman' more than once from the crowd. Some folk looked on disapprovingly, others nodded grimly. Two men got up from a table to shake Ramage's hand. An older woman shook her head then whispered something in his ear.

"I'll be fine, Henny," Ramage said, ruffling his hair bashfully. "Look who I'm with!"

A slap on the bar behind signalled Christian dropping off a pouch of provisions. "Ramage," the troubled man hissed, "what are you doing?"

"Going along with 'em, Christian." The stout man grinned from ear to ear, his teeth were about the brightest things in the room. "Save a drink for me for when I'm back, eh?"

"You can't be serious?" Christian whispered, and not very discreetly.

"Come on, lads," said Marigold, finishing Haggar's second cup for him and wrapping an arm each around Ramage's and Pettar's shoulders. Ramage's were bigger. "Let's go and get our stuff." He'd decided that Pettar could join them. That last drink sorted *that* decision out for him: the lad needed some bloody experience. "Christian, be a good man and see to it that our rukhs are stabled somewhere nice and warm. I expect them to be in good health when we return. Just watch yourself around those beaks though, they're about as sharp as the birds' temperaments."

Chapter Two

SUMMIT'S UP

Marigold's hot piss carved a ravine into the drifted snow at the base of the mountain. White steam rose up, reflecting the bright light of twin moons *Master* and *Pupil* as the clouds above cleared. Marigold snorted the warm mist from his face.

"Shouldn't've had that third cup, should ya, Boss?" laughed Pettar. "This is you all the way to the top, now."

"Fuck off," Marigold muttered, tucking himself away as a pale-yellow dribble coursed its way through the snow to his boots. Third cup? He'd had seven or eight. Or nine. He hadn't been counting.

Marigold shrugged inside his jerkin and furs to loosen some heat, then blew into his hands for some more fleeting warmth. Cold was to be expected when snow covered the land. The night skies were clear and the moons shone silver, but by Greldin, there were better times to tackle a mountain. Well, that was his decision. First proper job as Chief. He'd gone and said they'd do it and there was no backing down now. His boys were all dressed well enough, but just how that would hold up high on a frigid peak remained to be seen. Marigold had climbed mountains before. Shit, he'd climbed mountains nobody else would dare even consider, but he usually did that on a *little* more than a whim, and the skinful of alcohol that had birthed that whim was waning. The snow was thick at the base, lying in heaps and covering what Ramage claimed was a path that led towards the first steps of the mountain. They took the local at his word, for any footprints were buried by recently fallen snow. Marigold gazed up into the night. What a mountain she was. Spitertind, as she was named. She wasn't one of those slow rising peaks, a child's charcoal drawing of a gently-sloped triangle, no, this hulking rock was a steep and craggy bitch. Nature's finest, rising almost vertically from the ground at points around Elsdale, a mountain where trees struggled to affix themselves at the base and gave up entirely before the halfway mark. It was the only peak in the immediate area, with no other supporting mounds to diminish her grandeur. Ramage confirmed that the slope was gentler on the northern face, but the journey to that point was a day or more away at best and that he only knew that from his grandpap's stories; he'd never been himself. Few remaining Elsdale folk had. A trip that way meant working through the woods and undoubtedly encountering the cult, much like every other hopeful escapee had. No, to the north surprise was lost and an ambush might well await. A short, sharp climb it was.

Short, being relative.

The mountain itself might be foe enough for any normal man, but each fellow in this procession was far more interested in what lay at the top. Marigold had his huge claymore, Sear, strapped to his back. She was heavy, but he'd grown used to her weight over the years, growing all the stronger for it. Two vials of flammable liquid chinked together on his belt. Not as many as he would have liked to have on him, but that fluid was becoming difficult to come by in the clan's current state. Sear was a blade with a hollow hilt and minute grooves etched along the blade below. The vials fit perfectly inside the hilt and, once cracked open, the fluid would leak down the blade and ignite as soon as sparks flew, which in a battle that Marigold involved himself in was very soon indeed. Sear would become a white-hot cut of flaming metal. That alone was often enough to send most men hightailing it in terror. Folk claimed it magic, some Pit-granted spell infused into Marigold's very being. Marigold detested magic, and any cunt that cast it, but he didn't mind his enemies believing that he had a firm grasp of it. Alongside his signature weapon, Marigold carried an assortment of daggers that hung from belt and boot, and a short axe in a loop on his belt. Magnus and Pettar had knives of their own, but Magnus – that rippling mass of muscle, and the tallest man Marigold knew – still preferred to use his fists where he could. Marigold was not a small man by any stretch of the imagination, but Magnus still managed to make him look average in height. Better to have as a friend than an enemy. Scorched Haggar brought up the rear with yet more knives and a greataxe; a big two-bladed bastard with curved edges either side and a vicious spike on top for when swinging wasn't an option. Newcomer Ramage walked ahead, leading the group up their severe ascent. A stout axe clung to his side and a crossbow hung over his back. An assortment of bolts jangled on his belt. Marigold wasn't a fan of crossbows. Too many moving parts. Too many things to go wrong when you wanted instant and guaranteed death for your opponent.

"Ramage!" Marigold called, loping through the mix of soft and crunching snow. Marigold spied a glimmer of worry in Ramage as he looked back over his shoulder.

"Er, yes, Marigold? Anything wrong there?"

"Nope, not at all." He dusted the powder from his arms and stomach, noting the trepidation on the new fellow's tongue. "Just thought I'd get to know you a little better as we climb, warm the bones, you know? Good to know who you'll be fighting with."

"Fighting. Yes, so there will be," he muttered.

"Alright then, but she's going to get steep soon, she will; you might want to save your breath."

"We'll worry about that when it's a problem."

Ramage shrugged. There were the beginnings of a grin on his face. Cocky bastard.

The pair joined a narrow path that wound upwards. Marigold plucked a bone-hilt dagger and jabbed it into the rough cliff at their side. A breadcrumb, should the clan need it.

"You do know the way, right? Ramage?"

"Oh yes, yes I do. *The Crystal Cult*," he spat the name, "they may have chosen to set up shop at the peak of a mountain, so they did, but they at least made sure there was a decent path to follow. After all, the bastards need to get down easily to come and steal more of our folk. Never been up it meself, but you can see them coming down on it in daylight, you can. That one back there," he nodded at a split in the track, "that's just a dead end."

"You say this cult have had most of your family?" Well, why not rile the man up a little? Get his blood pumping for a scrap.

"They've had all of it, they have. Me dear Ma's buried in the cemetery down in the town, but she's only buried because she stood up to Cecil. If she hadn't fought back, she'd be up there now." Ramage looked up into the snowy heights. "She's why folk don't raise a hand. Her an' all the other dead ones."

"Who's Cecil?" Marigold asked.

"Aye. Who *is* Cecil? Don't know much about that particular bastard meself and not seen him in some time, but he wasn't young when he clubbed me Ma with the hilt of his blade. Bashed her wee head in, so he did. Don't even know if the fella's still alive, but I'd very much like to bump into him again. Preferably with the sharp end of this." He patted the axe at his side. "Russel was his second, think he might've been his son or something. If nothing else, at least we've seen the end of that halfwit. He won't be ruining folks' lives anymore, so he won't."

No, he would not. And he may even have been the son of an even meaner bastard? No wonder Christian had finally come out of his shell. "I've got to ask, Ramage, why the fuck haven't you all just found somewhere else to live if you haven't dared to fight back?"

"You think we haven't thought about it? Like I said, some have tried. They're dead now, or taken, so they are. Plucked from the woods, from the hills. It's not just our houses they take us from. I don't know how the cult know, but whenever anybody tries to leave – even since the beginning, since it all started happening – Cecil, or Russel, or one of the other high ups, they're always there, blocking the way, forcing us back in. And the ones they take after they try to get out? They don't 'count' when it comes to their damned quota, and neither do visitors like you. They'll let you all in but they won't let you out. Just a bonus for their lord, so you are, whoever the fuck that is. Not seen *him* ever come down the from top, but he must be a terrible bastard to need all of those lives. Dark magic, I reckon. Nobody ever goes willingly, but even so I wish that I could clear the screams of those that tried to escape first from me poor mind. We've had to make it through countless nights listening to the helpless cries of bound friends and families as they're dragged up there to meet whatever doom the cult have in store them. Aye, the sounds travel down far too well, and they fucking know it. None of us know what happens up there, none of us have ever found a body, or seen anyone we know come back down dressed in those bloody blue capes. A couple of brave wee souls have tried to find out for themselves, not seen them again, neither. I don't know if it's luck or a curse that we have enough of us left to keep on going. Just dragging it out. So many nights I've just lay there wishin' it would all end."

Not a bad story, but Marigold felt like probing a little more. "Still, Ramage, you at least look like a man that can handle himself. And so did half of the men in your inn. A desperate man is a dangerous one indeed." Marigold rubbed his chilled hands together and blew into his palms to warm his nose. It really was fucking cold, as much as he was loathe to show it. "Why in the Pits've one of you not buried an axe in one of these cult heads yet?" By Greldin, he could feel the ice on his thighs.

"There are a lot of 'em, and not very many of us, if you put the two groups together." Ramage stopped to breathe deeply as the path took a sharp and steep turn to the left, rising onto a ridge that overhung the route scaled so far. "No point in any of us killing just Russel – well, you've saved us that bother now – or just one of them if it only means some other, meaner bastard takes his place. Elsdale needs to be rid of the whole damned lot, and I can't do that by meself. When I seen you and your men take those bastards down… first time I've had hope in a long time. I'm thinking, so I am, maybe, just maybe, we can do it with you."

Marigold bit his freeze-dried lip. Maybe the folk of Elsdale had enough restraint to realise they couldn't take the entirety of the cult on, but their chances were only becoming weaker with each visit from them. Just how many of these cultists were there? And what made

Ramage believe that the five of them were enough to take them on if there were really that many? On the strength of a bar fight? It seemed that this Ramage wasn't someone who was just going to throw his life away unless he knew that he could make a big difference to all of the lives back in the town. For now though, it was better not to become too enamoured with the fellow; he still had a fair chance of crumpling down in a broken heap when the first fight broke out. "Pity more of you don't think the way you do, Ramage."

"How high's this fucking thing?" Magnus shouted from some distance behind Marigold and Ramage.

"Shhh!" hissed Ramage as he glanced desperately to the cliffs overhead. Fine powder glinted in the moonlight. "If you don't bring the bloody snow down on us, you'll alert the cult, so you will!"

"Right, right," whispered Magnus. The powerful man lunged through the snow to catch up with the leaders. He made remarkably little sound given his breath-taking mass. "Keep yer fucking skins on," he told Ramage with a grin, "just wanted to know how long we've got till I can crack some skulls."

"We've a long way to climb yet, er, Magnus, is it?" Ramage said.

"Aye, friend."

"Right, well, we've a good few hours ahead of us, and the steepest parts're still to come. I mean, you can't have missed this peak from down below, eh? Spitertind's a monster, so she is. Doesn't matter whether there's a path or not, it's not a quick climb whichever way you slice it."

"Those cult shits are going to have some bloody legs on them then, aren't they?" he asked nobody in particular, staring up into the black and white abyss of snow and rock and night.

"I'd not really thought about it," replied Ramage.

"They will. Climbing hills and mountains, that's what you want to be doing if you want to get like this." Magnus strode in front, flexing his legs and arms. Even beneath the layers of fur, the sheer size of each bicep was clear. Magnus couldn't keep the look of satisfaction from his smug face as he walked backwards, watching Ramage's eyes widen in awe. The moons glowed on his already shiny head, lending a further air of magnificence to the man. Confidence was one of the greatest assets in a barbarian.

Marigold slowed down as Ramage and Magnus took the lead, discussing the strength of the individual cult members that Ramage happened to know of. Sounded like a lot, but nobody stuck out like Russel and Cecil. Down below, only the tiny lights of the inn windows and small patches of snow marked out Elsdale. A bluish smoke rose from what Marigold guessed was the inn. Must be some sappy wood on the fire; that smoke would be seen for miles. There was a way to go yet, but even in the star and moonslight they were already high enough to see the far edges of the forest that encircled the entirety of the town and farmland. Haggar and Pettar were catching up, just approaching a twist in the path that would lead them onto the ridge that Marigold stood on. From what Marigold could make out, Pettar was talking non-stop at Haggar. Poor fucking Haggar. The man couldn't even tell the kid to shut up, and Pettar had an irritating penchant for spilling nothing more than Pit-spawned bullshit non-stop. The lad hadn't even seen twenty winters, how many wild tales could he reasonably expect people to believe? Especially stories vomited over people he had lived with his entire life. With luck, Haggar wouldn't kill Pettar before they all made it up to this Crystal Cult's headquarters. As the lagging pair drew closer, Marigold put his hands on his hips and stared up. The peak was still hidden. The worst thing about climbing mountains were the false summits. You quickly got it into your head that the hard work was done, and that the view, or wizard, or beast was just ahead, and then you saw another pissing mound rising up beyond it. What was it with high places and evil? Wizards in their towers, kings in their keeps, beasts up trees, and now a kidnapping cult up a fucking mountain! Was it a personality thing? Did the height give them a sense of grandeur they could never get on the ground?

Fucking cults.

Marigold had lost count of the number of times he had smashed a heart-pounding climb before some action, though he had to admit he quite enjoyed the build-up. "Come on, you sluggish cunts," Marigold chided Pettar and Haggar, "less talking, more walking! Ramage and Magnus'll be at the top of the bastard by the time we-"

The quaking began abruptly.

Bass notes groaned from deep inside Spitertind, in the rock and earth beneath the snow. White dust cascaded into the night sky as Marigold found himself flat on his arse. He watched helplessly as Haggar and Pettar both slid back down the twist they had just climbed. The shaking became stronger, more violent, as if the mountain itself had had enough of the cult and was ready to just shake them off. Marigold couldn't focus, everything moved too rapidly to understand. The rumbling rose, travelling up through the titanic formation of rock. A great crack blared out from above. Amidst the din, Marigold heard a tiny voice yelling, the words lost for good. The moons were removed from the sky as a dark shelf cut into the air. Marigold scanned left and right in panic. Everything shook so much he couldn't determine where safety hid and death lay waiting. He pushed himself back hard, against the cliff face behind him. Sear bit into his back as he took the best cover he could beneath the narrow lip of rock above. A slim chance, and he knew it. The shelf of packed ice and snow crashed down around Marigold, shattering into thousands of chunks. Down it all went, carrying on its descent as it created a new roar in the night.

"Haggar! Pettar!" Marigold was lost within din.

The rumbling from within the mountain rose up, thinning out as it travelled further. The shaking began to subside. Marigold focused on white knuckles that gripped useless holds in the snow around him. His knuckles stopped moving. The mountain stopped moving. Without a moment to check himself over, Marigold threw himself at the edge of skinny path, searching frantically in the snowy mass below that buried the path they had been climbing moments before.

"Haggar! Pettar!"

No response.

"Marigold!" Magnus cried out from somewhere further up.

No time to reply, Magnus was safe, or was at least alive. "Haggar, you cunt! Where are you? Say something!" Marigold swung his legs over the edge of the trail and dropped down onto the buried track below. Further than he had thought and the snow was so chopped up that it did little to slow his fall. Into the snow he plunged, the weight of Sear dragging him deeper still. Clinging, white snow enveloped him. Marigold's foot struck something hard yet yielding.

"Mmwhathefuck?"

Pettar. Thank fuck the irritating shit was still alive. Pettar was the wildcard in this group, and Marigold had only brought the pain in the stones along to Elsdale because Elvi, Pettar's sister, had asked him to. Perhaps it was early days that might not amount to anything more than that which had already come, but Marigold felt that he would do anything for Elvi, and that included volunteering to look after her headache of a younger brother. Oh, she knew. She knew that Pettar needed some toughening up, some adventures, some experience. That she had entrusted the lad to Marigold was good enough reason to believe that something more might be there. So really, the immature little shit *couldn't* be dead. He wasn't allowed to be.

The snow was close and heavy, inexorably pushing downwards as it began to settle again.

A lesser man would have given up and perished within this snowy tomb, but Marigold had fought his way out of packed snow before, and it had been thicker and deeper. He tightened his arms and heaved a great clearing within the snow around him. He set his boots against what might have been rock and reached down into the hazy, pale mass. He felt an arm. Marigold gripped and pulled with a force that he momentarily feared might rip the arm from the shoulder it was attached to. Greldin knew he'd managed that before. Up he yanked, and the brown hair of Pettar's head emerged from the depths. Soon, Pettar occupied the same makeshift snow cave that Marigold did. Steam rose from his shoulders.

"You were with Haggar, where is he?" Marigold shook Pettar.

"I'm fucked if I know, Marigold, you saw how hard that shitting snow hit! I hear the noise and the next thing I know I'm being buried alive!"

"Haggar!" Marigold yelled.

"Haggar!" Pettar called out.

"Haggar!" The pair roared together.

"Marigold?" Pettar panted.

"What is it?"

"Haggar's burned his fucking tongue out, hasn't he? Cunt might be right at our feet, he ain't gonna say anything."

"Fuck!"

The pair of them looked worriedly at each other. "Haggar!" They both called again.

"Chief! Pettar! Haggar!" Magnus was above. "Ramage, hold this. Here, grab it." A length of rope dropped into the top of the hole that the two barbarians occupied.

"Get yourself out of here," Marigold advised Pettar.

"What about-"

"I'll bloody find him. Bit of snow won't be the end of him, he'll just be a bit chilly."

Pettar was hauled out of the icy cavern as Marigold bent down, swiping yawning grooves through the snow to his left and right, digging deeper and deeper, as fast as his frozen arms would allow. The tunnel behind gently began to collapse, leaving just a covered space that followed Marigold within. Where the fuck was Haggar? Was he even on the path anymore? Had he gone over the edge? That wasn't a fall anybody was going to survive, not even fire-breathing, tongueless Haggar. Things were already getting desperate and they hadn't even found the fucking cult yet. Just what in the Pits had all that quaking been about? Marigold was going to find out, and he intended Haggar to join him in that. The barbarian chief twisted awkwardly within the snow to pull Sear from his back. He dragged her 'round to his front so he could see what he was doing with the hilt. Despite the ice surrounding him, the moons made the inside of the icy tunnel glow. Up was definitely still up, thank Greldin. Marigold fumbled at his belt and plucked one of Sear's vials free. He cracked the ice around the lid of hilt and slid the small capsule of metal, oil, and glass inside. With a twist of the mechanism, and some effort, he crushed the vial and spun Sear so that her tip faced down. Fuel slowly oozed down her grooves. He jabbed her with a small knife from his belt. Sear burst into glorious flame as Marigold recoiled within his tight quarters.

"Never know when your bite'll come in handy, eh?" he muttered to his beloved blade. Too bad she was eating snow and not flesh on this occasion.

The heat was intense, and right in Marigold's face. The snow above began to drip, hissing and spitting as it landed on the scorched metal. The fuel was hardy stuff and wasn't going to be extinguished that easily. Marigold pushed the blade into the snow. Steam burned his hands and cheeks. He closed his eyes and covered them with a palm as he carefully pushed the blade around. He didn't want to swipe too hard in case his mute friend really was just by him. Overhead, a small hole in the snow began to open up, revealing stars and moons and night sky.

"Haggar!"

Marigold pushed through. Something below his feet felt solid. The path. He slid his boots gingerly across the ground, feeling out for the edge of the path and the cliff. From within the snow, a dark shape loomed. A dark shape about six-and-a-half feet in height by Marigold's judgment. There he was, the frozen bastard, just sitting tight. Marigold propped his burning weapon in the snow and thrust both arms around the shape that had to be Haggar. Wet fur, chest, arms. It was him alright, and he was stone-cold. Marigold lunged once more and retrieved the barbarian from his snow prison. Heavy feet booted him in the face as he realised the poor fool had been upside-down the whole time. Thick arms wriggled and pushed themselves from the remainder of the snow. Haggar slumped down to the soft deck of the snowy hole. He pulled himself up and grinned in Marigold's face. Bright red blood streamed from his mouth. He flashed his teeth. The bastard was happy! Bloody Haggar. The man never took anything seriously.

"Y'alright?"

Haggar nodded.

"What about all that blood?"

The mute wiped a dismissive hand across his face.

"You're wet-fucking-through. Here, hold *her* for a moment, the heat'll help." Marigold passed Sear into Haggar's frozen hands. "What've you done to your mouth now? Here, let's have a look."

Haggar opened wide, and the light of Sear gave Marigold a decent view of the bloodied mess within.

"Fuck me, Haggar, your tongue really is gone. All of it. You're missing a few teeth as well. How's the pain?"

Haggar closed his mouth and nodded with a grimace. He held a palm out flat and wobbled it gently.

"Well, I did fucking tell you that you couldn't breathe fire."

Haggar made a start.

"Alright, alright, you did it, but you should have stopped after doing it once. Why'd you have to go and do it three times?"

Haggar agreed with a sad dip of his head. He scooped a handful of snow from the wall around them and popped it into his mouth. A smile of relaxation blanketed his face.

"How about we stop chilling our bones and get the fuck out of here?"

Haggar nodded eagerly.

"Ramage! Magnus! You got that rope handy? Hey! You hear us? We're down here. Oi!"

There was murmuring from above, but the snow fuzzed it up somewhat. The end of a rope dropped in through the hole that Sear's heat had been slowly widening.

"You first, Haggar."

"So, what the fuck was that all about?" Marigold asked Ramage when the five of them were safely out of the snow and warming themselves by the dying flames of the claymore. "Didn't you think it would have been a good idea to mention that the mountain likes to try and shake intruders off?"

"Now, now," Ramage quavered. His was a face clearly worried that a barbarian's anger might develop beyond words. "It's not happened very often, at least not *that* strong. Cult business, whatever it is. We've had quakes a few times before, so we have, but that *was* a bad one. Oftentimes it's no worse than a little purr."

"Well that was a fucking roar," Magnus said.

"This cult have got something special going on in there, haven't they?" Pettar asked. His eyes widened, lips curled up into a smile. He lunged on, ahead of the pack.

"Wasn't the snow enough? Cool your head, Pettar," Marigold dismissed. Fool was eager for a fight before understanding what it was they were facing. "Whatever it is, it's part of why we're up here, but we need to know what *it* is first. What is *it*, Ramage?"

"I don't know! Some cult magic? They don't tell us what they do up there. Who knows what those bastards are doing with our people."

"Fucking magic. By Greldin, of course it's fucking magic. You mentioned 'dark magic' before, know what type we're looking at?"

"Um, well, no, I-"

"Spells, charms, curses, demons. Magic's got it all, hasn't it? Can't go anywhere these days without some spell-chanting cunt getting up in your face. Well, Ramage, I'll tell you what, if there is magic at work up there," he jabbed a fist in the general direction of the centre of the mountain, "it's stopping today. Can't abide the fucking stuff. You want power, or wealth, or a fight? Use some damned steel, or your pissing fists. Shit, pay some coin if you have to, whatever that's worth. There's no room for magic where I'm concerned, and now I know it's there? Well, this little trip just became more interesting, that's clear."

Tirade over, Marigold stood up and strode off along the path ahead. His heart pounded. Excitement? Anger? A mixture of the two? He fingered his belt as he clambered away from his men. He'd only brought two vials for Sear, and he'd wasted one already melting the fucking snow. It was time to hope that nothing up there was immune to plain old steel, which *had* happened before. Ending the lives of magic users was one of Marigold's favourite pastimes and it made him feel truly alive. Drawing Sear from an expiring wizard or witch was a rush that couldn't be matched; watching the look of terror in their eyes as the pricks finally realised that their magic didn't make them invincible was something hard to beat. But there was still a note of uneasiness about tackling them, and there was also the matter of getting to the fight itself. You never knew what a spell-caster knew till they decided to cast it down upon you. Hard to plan ahead when you don't know what's coming. Moving a mountain? That was a new one for Marigold. "With luck," he looked up as he spoke at the mountain, "that'll be the first and last surprise we get. With even more luck, there'll be something dead beneath my feet by the end of the day." But what were they going to have to fight through to get there? Marigold's thoughts were interrupted by the others that were treading carefully behind him. Seemed they were wary of passing by, or at least Ramage wasn't letting them. The local was going to have to grow some bloody stones and do it at some point: Marigold didn't know the damn way beyond the direction of up.

"Is he alright?" Ramage whispered. Marigold heard it, regardless.

"The Chief don't like magic," Magnus said simply, "in case that wasn't bleedin' obvious enough. Had some bad experiences with it when he was younger."

"Oh."

"Ach, don't worry about it. He'll be excited more'n anything else, whatever he says. He does enjoy murdering folk that play around with the stuff. Really, it's sort of his thing. Ain't that right, Chief?"

"Too fucking right, Magnus," Marigold called back.

Ramage winced, while Pettar laughed his screechy, immature cackle.

Marigold navigated a particularly narrow stretch of rock with all the ease of a mountain goat. He was no stranger to a climb and hopped over a crack that looked to have been newly formed by the avalanche without any hesitation whatsoever, despite the gaping chasm below. His fingers slid into spaces between the rocks like they had long known the passage being taken. Some folk used ropes for climbing like this, Marigold preferred to trust himself. Magnus straddled the gap, a huge, booted foot planted on each side. Weapons were passed across, then Magnus lent Ramage a hand and hauled him over the gap. Ramage yelped as he looked down, much to the enjoyment of Magnus. In Marigold's opinion, the woodcutter's bravado was quickly running out and he hadn't even had to fight yet. With Ramage across, Magnus helped Pettar, who in turn helped Haggar. The five of them slung their gear over their backs once again and continued their ascent, grasping icy rock with bare fingers, and wedging furred boots into ragged footholds. After a few minutes of climbing in silence, Marigold stopped to gaze over the edge of the snow-covered trail once again. The wind whistled through the rocks, flecks of snow slapped his face. Elsdale was there below, a tiny orange dot, still with a smudge of blue smoke overhead. He opened up one of the packs of dried meat and chewed thoughtfully.

"Everything alright, Boss?" Pettar asked.

"I need a piss."

"What did I tell you about all that drink?" Pettar laughed.

That teenage guffawing grated something chronic between Marigold's ears. "And what *did* you fucking tell me? Got more experience with ale than I have? No. I just need a damn piss, Pettar. I've had half a mountain come down on me and my bladder would like to empty itself. Why aren't you pissing? Did you finish those cups or did you just pour them over the counter?"

"Just let him take his leak, Pettar," Magnus said, grabbing the youngster's shoulder and dragging him on.

Pettar continued laughing, though it was more forced than it had been before.

The group carried on with the climb. Marigold hung back, watching over the land. His eyes fixed themselves on the trees and snow and town. The forest really looked a lot bigger than it had seemed down on the ground. It was positively vast. Had they just missed the cult? Had they really been waiting for his group to reach the town? Perhaps the folk were so scared of leaving they missed each opportunity to escape as it arose. Forced to become weekly sacrifices? What a fucking life. Wouldn't have started in the first place had Marigold been there to begin with. And what of this mountain? Was it actually trying to get up and walk off? What was inside? Oh, there was magic involved alright. *The Crystal Cult*. Did they call themselves a cult, or was that Elsdale's name for them? What had Christian called them? *The Crystal Order*? Whatever, the pricks had to know they were on the wrong side. The evil side. Kidnapping and presumably killing these men, women, and children.

Marigold ground his teeth. It would all come to an end sooner or later. The sooner the better, as far as he was concerned.

Chapter Three

MORNING MASS(ACRE)

The pale reds of dawn lit up the snow around Marigold and his men. Ramage directed the group up the final slopes of the mountain, urging silence while Magnus continually cracked his knuckles and grumbled wordlessly. Stars that had shone so brightly a short time ago winked out one by one as the new day's sun claimed the skies. Crunching snow and wheezing lungs were the sounds of *this* morning.

"Y'know, this didn't seem like a bad idea at the bottom," hissed Magnus. "Not so fucking sure about it now. I'll barely be able to swing a fist once we reach the top."

Marigold slapped a palm to his face and dragged it over his nose. "Wasn't aware you were walking on your arms, Magnus, or are you an ape now? I understood you were made of sterner stuff. Now I'm thinking those cultists might be one better..." He sped up to aid his point, which didn't lessen the bite of the hangover he was eager to hide.

"Aw, fuck off, Chief," grumbled Magnus.

"Not far to go now, my friends. No, no, no, not far at all," whispered Ramage, leading the line. "Not been up here myself before, so I've not, but the way this ridge juts out..." he waved a finger across a wind-cut mass of black stone that broke through the snow. The slab arced over a great drop to the tiny path far below, "...that's Spitertind's Nose," he sniffed, "no doubt about it. Only the head – the peak – is left, so it is. Path's still going, too, can't be far." Despite being the apparent weakest among hardened barbarians, Ramage was the only one not out of breath. Marigold wasn't exactly having trouble himself – this was hardly the first mountain he had climbed – but he hadn't expected Ramage to be faring better. Most disappointing. There was going to be some serious training for him and the lads once they had their camp set up in Illis. Perhaps some morning runs up the soon to be cultless Spitertind would be in order.

A biting wind picked up, curling around the men as it squirmed between the furs and skins, nipped at clammy flesh. The barbarians blew into fingers cupped over noses, thrust hands under armpits. Ramage remained unaffected.

Perhaps Marigold would direct those future runs from the foot of the mountain.

"Arseholes had to make their base right up the pissing top, though, didn't they?" Pettar whined from the back of the procession. "I'm freezing my fucking stones off."

"It's just moan, moan, bloody moan from you babies, isn't it?" Marigold snapped. He was damn sure he was just as cold as everyone else, but was he whining about it? Not vocally. "You're lucky you've lost your pissing tongue, Haggar, because if you started bawling as well I'd be chucking the lot of you back down the way we've come."

"You're in some mood, eh, Chief?" Pettar asked, with a smirk on his face. "Wanting to shout a bit so you can pant without looking worn out? Thought we were meant to be quiet?"

Marigold watched Ramage's eyebrows raise in a pleading manner. The Chief didn't open his mouth but scrunched his fingers tight enough that the cracks snapped out over the chilled peak. Fucking Pettar. He wasn't wrong. Pettar was young, cocky, but above all, he was just downright annoying. Pettar thought he had something to prove, and it was all because he was less experienced in life than Magnus or Haggar or Marigold. With luck it was just his age. A few more jobs would see him grow out of these irritating characteristics and become more like a proper member of the clan. That said, Marigold didn't remember being quite like this back when he'd had fewer than twenty winters under his belt, and he knew that he'd been a shit himself at times. He took a deep breath, doused the anger. It was all for Elvi. He breathed deeply. Elvi was older than Pettar, tall – almost as tall as Marigold – raven-haired, and had a pretty little scar over her lip that curled her smile into a sarcastic sneer. He intended to discover how she had earned that, but there hadn't been much chance for talking yet. Elvi could fight with the best of Marigold's men, had a deliciously sharp tongue, and did things with the rest of her that Marigold just couldn't shake from his mind. He coughed into the mountain air as though he was under suspicion from the men around him. Well, once the clan had settled... maybe then he would take the next step. Maybe there would be no more secrets. Unless, of course, he ended up murdering Pettar first. That would probably kill things dead where they were, and Marigold was a man that was good at killing. His mind wandered to the night before travelling to Elsdale. As he grinned to himself, he thanked Greldin silently that Elvi didn't share any of Pettar's facial features; that would have ruined everything.

As the sun claimed more of the horizon, Marigold's mind returned to the situation at hand. Daydreams of his girl faded back into solid irritation at her little brother. And where had that annoyance really come from? A night of drinking and a decision made, regardless of how misguided it was. Eight drinks? Maybe nine? The local mix was strong. Stronger than he had expected.

The faint path widened out, footprints of differing sizes lay frozen in the icy crust. Ramage crept along, glancing at his feet and visibly balking at the sheer number of boots that had evidently trodden the peak. A place of business, of lookouts. And what a lookout. Views for leagues. Illis spread out below with its small collections of buildings far and wide, copses and rivers and lakes here and there, and above all, the plains and ridges that had drawn Marigold to the land. The morning sun cast dark shadows that cut the land up into chunks between the woodlands and rocks. So much more to explore, and somewhere down there the clan were waiting to do it on his command.

Back on Spitertind, large stones made rudimentary steps over the remaining rise to the summit. Less snow here on account of the land being used more frequently. But where were they? A good scout remained hidden but would have some other method of alerting his men. Marigold scanned for anomalies, the slightest movement. He didn't want the game to be given away now. A great mound of jagged, black and grey stone formed the eventual peak, while the trail wound around flatter sections that were shaded by it. Rocks like fingers reached into the sky, hinting at a once grander height for the mountain. Ahead, Ramage came to a stop, crouching behind a small, snow-capped boulder. Immediately, Marigold followed suit and ducked behind his own, smaller rock, gesturing to the others to do the same.

"What you got?" he hissed to Ramage.

Ramage mouthed something that Marigold couldn't make out. He held one open palm to the barbarians while his other hand jabbed wildly ahead.

This wasn't going to get them anywhere. Marigold checked for eyes on the uneven horizon and crept over to the man. As he slunk into the shade of Ramage's makeshift hideout, a straight-edged object emerged from behind the rocky points of the peak. Vertical, precise. A building. Marigold traced the edge up to where it met another, slanted side.

The hideout of the cult.

As no arrows had yet pierced his face, Marigold granted himself a full view of the structure. A squared bottom, with snow drifts pushed up against the walls. Empty, rusted sconces dressed with icicles flanked riveted doors of dark wood that were set in the middle of the wall. Both doors had a curious rectangular image etched onto them, worn somewhat where the wind had eaten away at them. The stone was dark, almost black. The edges of the bricks at the corners were jagged, spitefully cut by the savage weather of the peak. Everything about the building spoke of viciousness – more monster than structure – and this somehow raised Marigold's expectations of the cult members within. The construction was capped with a triangular rooftop. Jagged slates clung to the sides, many missing, most covered in snow and ice. A broken weather vane twisted and screeched in the winds atop a small spire over the door side. Some kind of tube shape adorned the top of it, similar to the doors. Eager to see what the rest of the building looked like, Marigold shuffled around the rock, sliding fingers so as not to lean too far. The roof led back to a second spire. Taller than the first, and with a great brass bell hanging in an opening near the top of the walls.

No doubt about it, it was a fucking church. A church that someone had deemed fit to build almost at the very peak of Mt. Spitertind. By Greldin's perfectly-formed stones, what poor bastards had been forced to lug the materials for that all the way up here? The good folk of Elsdale?

It was always the same with these crazy, religious zealots. They always had to focus on a place, usually high up, usually in some elaborate building. The church itself wasn't exactly some incredible feat of architecture, but it had been built in the most ridiculous of places. It said a lot about the self-importance of the arse-wipe behind the cult. Greldin didn't give a toss whether you thought of him while you ate, slept, travelled, or took a shit, but Marigold was willing to bet that if you were part of this so-called Crystal Cult, you worshipped at the top of the damn mountain or not at all.

"Cunts," Marigold spat into the snow.

"Sorry there, Marigold, you alright?" Ramage whispered.

"Aye."

Haggar, Magnus, and Pettar had all arrived around the small rock by the path, and, truth be told, it was having some difficulty hiding five large men.

"Doors're shut, nobody's outside. Doesn't look like we've been seen," Marigold told the men.

"I'd make it seem that way too if I wanted to ambush someone, so I would," Ramage muttered.

"Nah," Magnus broke in. "We all saw Russel and his men back down in the inn. Full of 'em selves, weren't they? Not the kind of folk that'd sneak about. They're all about bein' right in your face, showin' you who's boss. None of them up here know we're coming, 'n' if they did, I reckon they'd have confronted us by now."

"Aye, you could be right, I s'pose," Ramage said, shifting back a little to allow the warriors to get their looks in. "All I really know of these bastards is what they do back down in our wee little town."

"What we need to do now is get in there as quietly as we can," Marigold said. "It could be fucking empty for all we know, or there could be men inside. Lots of men. If this cult's as big as you say it is, Ramage, that building doesn't seem big enough to hold even half of them, and there's also the folk they've taken from Elsdale."

The wind rushed over the church towards them, carrying the sounds of chanting, male voices. Not empty, then.

"They'll all fit if they're in there arse to face," Pettar sniggered.

"Will you shut it, you idiot?" Marigold snapped.

Haggar swiped his hand across the back of Pettar's head with a clap louder than Marigold would have liked.

"Oh, fuck you! Fuck you all! Fuck the fucking lot of you," Pettar cried out. "Always giving me shit because I'm younger than all o'you." Pettar stood up from behind the rock, head and shoulders in full view of anybody that *might* be watching. He stared intently at the church. "I'll fucking show you, Chief. And you Magnus, Haggar. I'm no weaker than any of you right now. You're old, I'm young. You're pissing about over things that haven't even happened when you all need to just get to it. Watch how it's done." And with that, the shitting upstart stormed off in the direction of the building.

"Get back here this fucking instant," Marigold hissed through gritted teeth. Was he calling to a teen or a five-year-old? A chief shouldn't have to put up with this idiocy. Barbarians were better than this. What in the Pits must Ramage be thinking about them? Rabble? Disorganised? No respect? By bloody Greldin. "Pettar!"

But Pettar was gone, and he clearly had no intentions of turning back. After all, he was trying to prove himself. Trying in the most stupid manner possible. He wasn't going to get anywhere if he showed himself up to be nothing more than hot air, and Marigold knew it.

"It's not how I'd liked to have done this," Marigold quietly addressed the group, "but that infantile fucker isn't coming back. If we don't follow him now he's going to get himself killed and that'll put us at the disadvantage." Not to mention ruin things with Elvi. Marigold started up from behind the rock and began pacing deliberately over the snow and stones on the path to the church. Crunching feet echoed as metal slid from leather. A dagger, to begin with. "Come on," he whispered back, gesturing at the others to follow. "Let's just hope there aren't many of the bastards in there."

Magnus and Haggar were behind Marigold in an instant. Haggar held his enormous axe between his hands, his fingers only just long enough to wrap themselves around the thick haft. Magnus was flexing his digits, curling them into fists and then stretching the tips. The man was more than ready for some fighting.

Marigold only heard two sets of feet behind him and shot a glance back to see an anxious Ramage fiddling with the bolts for his crossbow. The man looked panicked. Probably his first fight. He hoped to Greldin that the local was a good shot; if Marigold ended up with a bolt in his back there'd be a bloody price to pay.

Pettar was already at the doors. The lad may have been young but he was undoubtedly strong. His fur overcoat stretched taut as his muscular arms gripped the black metal loops fastened to the door. Pettar heaved and a spray of powdered snow arced by his sides. The doors groaned as they fell outwards. The chanting halted.

"Russel, you're... You're not Russel."

Here it was. The surprise.

Marigold snatched a shot at Ramage. Quivering. He'd better not be pissing himself.

"Men, to arms! Intruders at the doors. For our Lord! For the Will of the Worm!"

The will of the what? There was no time to think on that now. Marigold was mere strides from the threshold when four blue-cloaked men burst from the entrance. Pettar thrust his knife straight into the throat of the first, but the dying man had been skewered while flying at some speed. Pettar was shoved down to the snow beneath the dead weight *he* had created, a mere breath into the fight. A spurt of blood painted the fool's face, spreading across the white snow as he rolled to avoid a long blade from the second blue-cloak right above. Sparks flew where the weapon struck stone instead of flesh. Up the sword went, ready for another attack. Before it fell again, Marigold's dagger left his hands and found a new home between the ribs of the fellow. The longsword clattered harmlessly to the stones of the church entrance, but the blow wasn't enough to down the owner as well. Marigold rushed in and finished the job, thrusting his palm into the protruding hilt and sending the red, pointed end tearing through the other side. The poor man's eyes widened as he slumped down. Pettar was saved from a doom of his own creation, for now.

Marigold's crew joined in and the skirmish began in earnest.

Crunching snow, eager breaths, ringing metal. Cries of confusion barked, the words lost amongst one another. The cult were in a panic, but a third man leapt forward and tried to make something of it. Magnus's fists smashed an eye right out of his head. The orb stuck fast in the snow as the owner fell with it like the weight of the world dragged him down. The sorry bastard clutched at a short length of sinew and nerves that trailed from the empty socket. One side of Haggar's axe embedded itself within the chest of the fourth man, effectively ending the first assault from the church. The next wave wouldn't be so eager. Haggar jerked at his weapon to free it as the wind curled around him and threw the gross squelching inside the building.

"Keep at them! Attack! Don't let them through!" the directing voice inside was old, terrified, bewildered.

Marigold spied the source: an ancient, grey-bearded man in a blue robe. Not a fighting man. A gold-trimmed headdress wobbled precariously atop his age-lined brow. Beside the elder were at least ten more armed cultists that formed a protective circle around their man, and beyond them were a collection of unarmed men and women. They scrambled up from behind the priest – or whatever in the Pits he was – and began to file away into a black space at the far end of the dingy interior. A fucking escape route with the echoes of steps and the promise of darkness. The old man's arms were raised, jabbing this way and that, attempting to conduct the chaos that was to form the remainder of this impromptu defensive.

Ramage appeared at Marigold's side on the doorstep. The woodcutter took barely a heartbeat to aim before firing his crossbow. The bolt struck true, embedding itself in the space between the priest's mouth and nose. Ramage seemed just as surprised at the hit as Marigold was. The Chief briefly studied the local amidst the furore. Was that a good surprise or a bad one? Had he meant to miss? Nevertheless, the feathered shaft quivered in the bloodied face as teeth and globs of blood burst out at the sides. It was enough to send the old fool crashing into his lectern but the bastard quickly scrambled back up, minus his headwear. The priest was almost entirely bald save for a few wild strings of white hair. No doubt the churchman was just as amazed at his survival as everyone else in the room. Ramage swore loudly and dropped to a knee, "Damn it all," he cried, entering into a desperate struggle with his next bolt.

He dropped it.

Marigold growled and charged into the vestibule, scraping his foot over the missile. Too hard. The small shaft of wood and metal clattered over the snowy stones and out of reach. More men broke off from the circle. In they rushed, terrified yet determined to push the intruders back. Marigold locked into arm-on-arm struggle with one as two others directed themselves at Magnus and Haggar. Ramage scrabbled about on all fours, lurching for the dart as barbarian and cultist kicked it between themselves. Marigold roared in his attacker's face, spit flecking the terrified man's eyes. He just needed everyone to get inside. Marigold's forehead cracked the enemy skull as it leaned in too closely, all the while the Chief kept one, glaring eye on the bolt as it bounced around the flattened and bloodied snow. Only the second one – just one fucking fumble - and already that Pit-fucked weapon had become the problem Marigold always knew it would be. Honestly, who brought a ranged weapon to an unplanned skirmish? The man had an axe on his belt! Was it exclusively for trees? Finally, the woodcutter managed to lay fingers on the projectile. It was a wonder the imbecile hadn't felt a blade slide through his back already.

Pettar was up again and barged past, knocking the bolt once more from Ramage's hands while shoving Marigold off-balance in the process. That was the opening the Chief's concussed foe needed, and fists rained down onto ribs. Meanwhile, the fucking upstart barbarian charged right into the church alone, again! Pettar was simply uncaring of the seven men eager to put blades against him, clearly choosing to forget that that very same approach had almost seen him dead mere moments before. Pettar threw himself into the air with a guttural cry and thrust another blade into the throat of the priest.

Marigold found his feet and smashed a knee into the stones of his cultist. Hard enough that the man was out like a light. He stomped on the head and rushed into the church. Pettar was fast becoming far more trouble than he was worth, and if he didn't start to vary his attacks, each and everyone one of those cultists was going to know his next move. "Get in here," he yelled to Haggar and Magnus. "Ramage, in you get."

All quickly complied and the vestibule was emptied. No more pissing about on the threshold. Welcome or not, Marigold and his men were breaking in and doing what they came to do. Magnus chose a new target, while Haggar swung his axe through the necks of three cultists at once. The off-white walls of the church were quickly bathed in hot, red blood. Ramage, the last of them, stumbled over the threshold as he finally drew the string back on his weapon.

"This is a lock-in!" Marigold cried, slamming the doors shut and thrusting the sword of the man he had felled through the inside handles. He sincerely doubted that anybody was going to come in, but he didn't want anybody getting out either.

A deafening peal bawled out from above the ceiling. Barbarian and cultist alike staggered back and forth as the vibrations shook their skulls. That fucking bell in the spire was being beaten by someone. So much for a surprise attack. So much for a shitting stealthy approach! It was going to be cultist diarrhoea from here on in. Just Marigold's fucking luck. What Chief had ever let a battle fall apart so quickly? Not one destined to lead for long, that seemed to be certain.

Ears adjusted. Weapons were steadied and directed at foes once again. At least the bell had knocked the enemy off balance as well. Haggar kicked at a nearby pew and shattered it, sending the dark-haired man near him reeling backwards in a shower of splinters. The doomed bastard never stood up again as Haggar's axe came down on him whilst he still struggled amidst the fragments.

Marigold counted six capes. The bell continued to sound. Had more arrived on the scene?

Pettar was clinging to the back of a particularly tall, yet skinny man with long blonde hair tied back in a ponytail. Magnus was throwing heavy punches at Blondie's face as Pettar held him more or less in place. Blondie's left eye was already a swollen mess and his jaw hung at a broken angle; dead or not, he probably wished he was. Magnus threw one more blow to his right cheek, and Pettar twisted his neck with a snap. Sorted. Both Pettar and Blondie fell in a heap. Pettar needed to work out what those bloody feet of his were for, the lad had spent more time on his arse than off it so far. As Magnus grinned and clapped his hands at the violence, a shorter, ginger-haired fellow ran knife-point-first into his side.

With a cry to rival the bell, Magnus spun on the spot — knife sticking out of his side — and kicked so hard at the diminutive man that the snap of his back could be heard above the din. Ginger folded backwards and collapsed to the stone flags below with a hissing sigh. Magnus wrenched the knife out of his side. The spray of blood reached Marigold's face. A dark, tousle-haired man with one eye seemed to think that the massive barbarian's wound would make him an easy target, and charged directly at the giant. It was an unfortunate move for the fellow, as Ginger's knife soon found itself wedged directly through Tousle's temple, sending the eyes below sliding off in opposing directions. A curiously bloodless execution, that one.

Only three remained, and they'd cleverly formed a wedge formation at the back of the church to guard the shadowy hole that the unarmed cultists had fled through. Say what you will about the sheepish tendencies of cult members, nobody told these men to do what they were doing and here they remained, facing certain death. Longswords were held out, sharp, deadly, and ready to stab. Pettar was closest, but the fool was unarmed; the least well-equipped to be taking any of them on, physically or mentally.

Marigold cast Pettar aside like he was some willowy branch. He heard the beginnings of rabid fury spewing from behind as he set to tackling the three cultists alone. Not heeding his own advice perhaps, but as Chief he was clearly in a position of 'do as I say, not as I do' and he knew that he was more than capable of the task. The men may have been armed and holding formation, but there was little conviction in the wavering limbs that held the blades. Marigold smoothly drew Sear from his back, smashed the swords from the hands of the two either side of him, and ran the whimpering man in the middle through. The impaled man's sword fell onto Marigold's shoulder then clattered harmlessly to the deck as Marigold pushed his face close to his victim. Magnus and Haggar arrived either side of Marigold to snap the necks of the other two.

The bell continued to ring desperately, but no further forces were coming through that dark tunnel.

"Do something about that fucking noise, will you, Magnus?" Marigold yelled, drawing Sear from the cultist.

"Aye, boss man," Magnus replied, and disappeared through the narrow hole at the back of the church.

"No, get away from me!" a voice from within the shaft wailed.

The sounds of limbs slapping cold stone repeatedly slipped out from the dark doorway. They were punctuated by a loud crack and a deep laugh.

The bell stopped ringing. Wind whistled through the hastily locked doors at the front of the church. Ramage's chattering teeth became the loudest sound in this desecrated place of worship as the last gasps of men struggling to hold on to life drained away. Blood spattered the uneven floors, the mouldy walls, and dripped quietly from the dark rafters above. So much for a stealth attack, this little battle had become a bloodbath. Not something Marigold and his men were averse to, generally, but there was a time and a place for shit like this.

At the very least, there was some calm at last.

Marigold wiped Sear on his arm and dropped her back into her sheath. He looked down at his feet as he shifted them. The old priest's face stared wide-eyed towards the ceiling, bolt still wedged firmly between his gums. An arm appeared on the pew alongside Marigold.

Pettar. The youngster pulled himself to his feet and walked purposefully into the aisle towards Marigold, his mouth began to open.

Marigold threw his fist into Pettar's nose with a crunch. "Fine fucking job you did there, idiot!" Marigold roared in his face. Blood bubbled from Pettar's nose, the skin around it seeming all the whiter for it. "Were you actually trying to get us all killed, or did you just think that your little stunt would go without a hitch? You didn't even know what this fucking building held inside it! What'd you've done if a fucking team of skags had been on the other side? Or if a tripwire had sent a bolt your way? Or my fucking way?"

"I-I..."

"Nothing more from that mouth, Pettar. Magnus has a fucking hole in his side; you're lucky the bastard's all muscle or you'd have a dead friend's blood on your hands. Fuck knows how Haggar is, bastard couldn't even tell us if he was injured!"

"Aaaooowaaaye," offered Haggar, shrugging. Blood began to leak from between his lips with the effort.

"It's probably better if you *don't* try to speak right now, eh Haggar? Really ruins the fucking point I'm trying to make." Marigold locked eyes with the hot-headed youngster. "It might come as something of a surprise to you, Pettar, but thinking first about things is a damned good way to make sure you come out breathing on the other side of whatever it is you're getting yourself and your crew into. You carry on the way you are and you'll last less time than a rukh fart in a strong wind. You learn in a fight so that the next one goes better. Don't think about how much you want to hate these folk you're fighting, you don't know them! You're not going to get to know them because once you've killed one you're onto the next. Just remember, Pettar, you actually need to be alive in the next fight to put to use what you learnt in the last.

"Now, you can stay behind us or you can go back to the fucking clan. I don't want to see or hear any more shit from you for the rest of this job. You're here to learn, so fucking take all of this as a lesson and bloody remember it!"

Pettar didn't reply.

Now that some semblance of order was beginning to return to the scene, Marigold found himself with a moment to take a better look at his surroundings. What had appeared to be nothing more than a generic church began to reveal the idiosyncrasies that made it a definitive part of the *Crystal Cult*. Iron ornaments of a cylindrical design stood on the white windowsills below stained-glass windows. Marigold traced a finger along the lead lining between white and yellow cuts of glass. A large, crystal-blue shape that hung in the middle of each window. Not quite a rectangle, the blue glass tapered as it reached up to the top of the window. The glass was dirty and scratched from years of being beaten by the wind outside, but Marigold could see the dark shape of Spitertind's shoulders reaching out to the north-west.

Pews of dark wood were scattered at all angles now that the skirmish was done with. Each was carved in intricate detail; etchings of men crouched before that same large tower-like object. Same as the bloody window, the doors, the weather vane. Well, where was this idol tower? It wasn't in Illis that was for sure, Marigold would have noticed an eyesore like that. Were they worshipping a phallus here? He'd come across worse in his time... He leaned in for a closer look, gripping the edge of the wood. The piece of damp furniture creaked and groaned, moulding beneath his huge hands. He squeezed and tore, ripping off the corner of the pew like it was a wet pie crust. No longer did Haggar's feat of shattering one with his shin seem so impressive. Marigold opened his palm to look at the contents. Tens of minute, white grubs writhed within the flakes of wood. He cast them to the floor in disgust and ground his boot over them. How these things managed to hold a resting arse was anybody's guess. Marigold looked around at the rest of the church. One of the pews was managing to hold up Ramage's backside, at any rate.

"Hey, Boss," Magnus boomed, crouched in the small door at the back of the church.

"What's the matter, Magnus," Marigold asked, still brushing flakes of wood and worm from his palms.

"Got the arsehole up top, throttled him with 'is own bell cord," he laughed, "but there ain't nobody else up there, and nowhere else to go higher anyway. Those other ones went down."

"There some cellar below or something?" Marigold asked.

"Some-fucking-thing," Magnus replied, curiously.

"Well, we're not leaving this cult to regroup, are we? Let's corner them in whatever room they've holed themselves up in and rid ourselves of the fuckers once and for all. They weren't armed, but they might have found something pointy down there. Haggar, Pettar, Ramage, come on, get yourselves together, we've work to do."

Magnus disappeared back into the depths, "Aye, Elsdale'll fucking love us for this. Might even get me one of those girls Haggar was holding on to." The giant was followed by a cautious Ramage, and Haggar, who grinned a bloodied smile at Marigold as he went past. Pettar took a pace forwards as the footsteps of the others became fainter.

"What did I say, Pettar? Stay behind or go home."

"Yes, Chief," said Pettar, standing aside as he let Marigold pass.

Chapter Four

THE CRYSTAL KEEP

"It's fucking dark," Magnus complained, trudging loudly down the staircase as it wound deep below the church. Into the unknown depths the group descended, the depths that this cult in the mountain called home. "Could be any prick waiting right in front of us."

Marigold could practically hear the man's grimace cracking his face. "All the more reason to seal those lips and keep an ear out for sharp points coming your way then, eh?" He was still bubbling over his lecture at Pettar. Had he sounded like he knew what he was talking about? Had he been fair? Had the boy taken the words seriously? It seemed more likely that he had just made an enemy.

The steps underfoot were uneven, as though they had actually been hewn in complete darkness without any understanding of the shape of what was being made. The space was narrow and suffocating, an escape route or a means to an end; this wasn't a proper thoroughfare, so where was another? Despite the claustrophobia, the increased warmth was at least welcome; the Chief actually had some hope that he'd feel his stones once again. He gave them a shake, just to confirm their presence remained.

Marigold's feet slipped on a step only half as deep as his soles were long. Out went his boot, punted into the arse of Haggar.

"Uaaaahoo," yelled the man.

"It's only my fucking foot!" hissed Marigold, desperately trying to save some semblance of face in this embarrassment.

Haggar's breathing eased.

Thankfully, that backside had steadied him from falling further. Marigold listened to the soft scrape of each man's palm on stone as they steadied themselves on the unseen steps. Anybody that had escaped down these without injury had descended them on more than one occasion. Just where were those pricks now? Waiting in the walls for a moment to strike? Marigold couldn't discount the possibility; cultists were rarely strongmen and favoured sneak attacks in the face of power as far as Marigold's knowledge of them ran.

"No..." Ramage muttered from some step below. "Can't go down that far, it can't."

From Marigold's point of view, it already had gone down *that* far. His excellent sense of direction wasn't just limited to fields and forests, and he'd counted ten full spirals since ducking into the dark stairwell. The twists were tight and steep; those ten full circles went deep. He loosened the furs around his neck. Of course, he was *too* warm now. If these steps twisted all the way back down to a cave entrance into Elsdale, then Sear would be lighting Ramage up before the cult even felt any heat.

"Oh, fuck," gasped Pettar from the back of the line.

A skid and a scrape of leather on stone swiftly became hot breath on Marigold's neck. Marigold was a man that could hold back a charging rukh, but he'd never tried anything like that on a downward flight of ill-cut, twisting steps in utter darkness. His boot gave up once again. Sear's hilt cracked him hard in the skull. An explosion of light burst into his eyes as he pitched down into Haggar. Haggar went to his knees and barged Ramage, Ramage was flung forwards into Magnus. Magnus yelled a string of obscenities that remained clearly audible over the five tumbling men. Finally, the man at the front – whoever that was at this point – came to a stop, a solid buffer for the others to roll into.

"Fuck me, you're just as much shitting trouble behind as you are in front!" Marigold groaned from the heap. He ran his tongue around his chewed cheeks and spat a mouthful of blood onto an arm that was in his face but wasn't his.

"I tripped! I couldn't see! I just-"

"By Greldin, it doesn't bloody matter, does it?" Marigold snorted. "We're at the bottom now. Saved ourselves some time I suppose."

"Nice one, Pettar," Magnus added.

"I'd rather have kept my shins," moaned Ramage.

Haggar remained silent, his mouth was no doubt paining him enough to mask any other injury he might have sustained in that little tumble.

"Alright, alright, we're all grown men here. Stop getting your cocks in a fucking twist," Marigold snapped, ignoring his own part in the argument. "Let's just pick ourselves up and get on with it." He was fuming but he'd slipped already himself and could hardly blame the lad for the same mistake. Wanted him to learn from this expedition, not be scared off from joining in with anyone else again. Elvi wouldn't be happy if Marigold brought back a brother that was broken. That aside, Marigold did briefly consider offing Ramage whilst under cover of pitch darkness; he certainly didn't want tales of his men fumbling their way through this job to spread across Elsdale and beyond, and he still wasn't entirely sure about that look on the woodcutter's face when he had shot the priest up above. He thumbed the hilt of a dagger on his belt but his benevolence got the better of him, as so often it had these last few years. After all, Ramage might genuinely have the accuracy of a one-eyed roughskin. Ten years ago, Ramage wouldn't have breathed again after dropping that crossbow bolt back up at the church doors. Marigold dropped the blade silently back into its sheath. There was still time to turn this embarrassment around.

The men gathered their bearings, fumbling on the stone underfoot for lost weapons to slot back into loops and scabbards. It was a wonder none of them had impaled themselves in the fall. The steps were done with, but there was still no light, still nothing to see. Marigold stretched his arms out, reached up. The space they were now in was wider than the staircase had been. The walls and ceiling were rough-hewn rock; man-made tunnels in the mountain rather than the defined walls of the expected cellar. Seemed this way wasn't to be over and done with just yet. On they shuffled, wary of another drop. The floor was smooth, small mercies. It wasn't quite flat, but gently sloping as it drifted further down into the mountain. Marigold and his men were locked into a downward journey it seemed. After all that fucking climbing, too.

"Reckon I cracked my fucking skull in that fall," Magnus grumbled from the front of the group. His voice travelled somewhat, echoing around the group. "Got some bloody haze in my eyes."

"It blue?" asked Pettar from behind.

"Er, yeah."

"I got it too," said the youth.

"So do I," said Marigold, rubbing his eyes with a palm. "It's not your head, the fucking walls are glowing."

"We fallen into the Pits, then, Chief?" laughed Magnus.

"Not likely, though you'd bloody love that, eh?" said Marigold, grasping at the damp blue fuzz on the walls.

"Well yeah, we might get a decent fight."

"Sorry to disappoint you, Mag. It's moss, or fungus or something. Here, look." He tore a clump from the wall and passed the handful to the shadowy shape of Magnus in front of him.

"Cheers." The huge man held it close to his face, where it lit him up ghoulishly. Magnus seemed positively enamoured with the stuff, passing it back and forth below wide eyes and between grasping hands as the group continued deeper into the mountain. He smacked his lips and spat in disgust. "It don't taste great."

"What? Why in the Pits are you eating the stuff?" Marigold asked.

"It's actually not inedible, you know," Ramage piped up. "This moss, it's Cerulean Hair so it is. Grows in the overhangs at the base of the mountain, a good beacon for the drunk as they stumble out of the inn. Stands to reason it'd grow well in here too, I guess. The stuff has its uses beyond helping you see in the dark though as it makes a rather strong spirit, isn't that right, Haggar?"

Haggar's confused grunt bounced around the cavern from somewhere behind Marigold.

"That liquor you drank at the inn, the one you breathed your flames with? That was Cerulean Spice," Ramage proudly explained.

Haggar grunted sadly.

"Well, we *do* tend to just sip at it, not set fire to it. Takes some of the edge off having your whole family taken and killed so it does, I suppose."

Haggar made a series of grunts and moans that covered agreement, anger, sorrow, and indifference.

"Hmm. I quite like it, so I do. In small measures."

"By Greldin's fucking axe, Ramage," Marigold cried, briefly surprised by just how far his voice seemed to travel. He continued with a calmer whisper, "We're down here, deep in unknown cult territory and you're banging on about moss and bloody drink."

"Just nice to have some familiarity to the place."

"Oh, I'm sure it fucking is. You want to lead the damn way?"

No response.

The light from the Cerulean Hair *was* a welcome relief though, Marigold had to admit. The further they walked, the thicker and brighter it became. Darkness didn't bother Marigold in the slightest, whether it was a starless night sky or a blindfold around his eyes and the headsman above, but being able to see more than nothing in a cave where blades might be poised at every step of the way was a pleasing development. The light had other uses as well, namely highlighting just how much the path was beginning to narrow down at foot level; darkness would have seen one of them trip themselves up again. Water dripped down from above. Cold drops in this otherwise balmy interior. Every movement cast tinny echoes inwards. Echoes that would undoubtedly reach the escapees and the expected greater force that was hidden somewhere. Marigold half believed they'd end up face to face with a group so bored of waiting they'd be stood tapping their toes in impatience. The trespassers couldn't have been quiet even if they wanted to be, splashing puddles, kicking stones, scraping rock. Chewing on Cerulean Hair...

As their eyes adjusted to the azure glow, the moss revealed a gaping expanse of open cavern ahead. No longer just a widening tunnel, the trail opened up, but only insofar as offering a grand view before certain death in exchange for a misplaced foot. While the roof overhead soared to the top of the deep insides of the mountain, the path itself took a sharp left turn, hanging over a drop so precarious that even Marigold hesitated to hold his gaze of it. The tunnel wasn't just deep, Mt. fucking Spitertind appeared to be almost entirely hollow. The doing of magic, no doubt. Marigold jerked as Magnus sniffed sharply at his side. The skinhead barbarian spat and the blue-white blob twisted and twirled as it faded into the depths of the abyss. That was some bloody drop indeed.

"Did you know it was like this in here, Ramage?" Marigold asked the local man.

"No. I didn't even know there was a church at the top, if I'm being honest," the woodsman answered, "let alone a path into the mountain itself. Only rapids rush out from the cracks in the bottom that I know of, so they do, nothing you can enter. You're gonna have to believe me on this one, sir. Water is powerful, you know? It does a lot to wear stone down. Maybe the snow from above has done all of this over the years."

"And cut the fucking steps out, too?" boomed Magnus, scraping the rock underfoot as he took the turn on the path. Pebbles and fragments tumbled over the edge, Magnus watched them in awe. "How many members d'you say this Crystal Cult has, Ram?"

"Never said I knew a number, Magnus, did you ever hear me say a number?" Ramage spat out. "Never said I knew a number, by Fyr, I didn't."

"Alright, alright. Fuck me."

Marigold noted *that* display of bravery.

"All I know is that there'll be far more down there than we killed up top. Seen three times the amount of faces between their visits down to the town, so I have. Where they've all gone though, that's anybody-"

"And just what the fuck do we have here?" Marigold interrupted, jabbing a finger into the opening space beyond.

A truly enormous, blue cylinder emerged from within the vast haziness of the cavern as the skinny path wound its way down. It was distant, but from the cliff they trod it was impossible to tell just how far away the curious object was. What *was* certain was that the bastard thing was enormous and it glowed brighter and bluer than any of the moss coating the walls. The structure appeared slightly narrower at the top than further down – or else that was a trick of the glow and shadows – and was seemingly built into the cavern roof, buried deep within jagged stalactites. Marigold scanned the anomaly. The radiance it exuded pulsed lazily, rising in bright, luminescent rings from bottom to top as if the damn thing was alive. By Greldin, just how fucking big was it? From his vantage point on this perilous path, the tower seemed every bit as large as the mountain that housed it. Marigold sighed a sigh of two halves: annoyance and interest. A Pit-cursed, shitting tower, down here inside the mountain! So Illis did have its wizards. Magic infected everywhere he bloody went, he couldn't escape the stuff, worming its way into even the darkest recesses of the land. At least he was here, on hand to snuff the fucking stuff out. He studied the tower in greater detail. No windows adorned the rounded walls of this particular building, but then why would anybody want to look outside into a cave?

"Marigold, sir, I-I-I didn't know anything about this, so I didn't," Ramage stuttered.

"Indeed. I reckon that's where our doomed cult has run off to," Marigold said through his grimace. The insignia on the church window *was* local, on the doors, the rotten fucking chairs… It was clear now what it was meant to depict. "No doubt it's the home of the sorcerous prick that shook the mountain earlier, too. Bet the cunt's sitting pretty at the top, twiddling his wand or his cock, whichever's more impressive. Maybe he's sat there with both in his hands, locked in perpetual indecision as to which one is the least pathetic. Fucking wizards! Just what in the Pits is going on with this particular arse boil? Who makes his home in a tower like this? When a magic-weaving wanker decides that living in a fucking mountain is the best choice available, you tend to expect the hidden lair to be a little less garish."

Sniggers fluttered, but Haggar's was bitten off with a partial sob. Haggar had long been a supporter of Marigold's tirades, siding with him no matter the argument, egging him on in an effort to increase the intensity of the verbal barrage. Marigold had to admit he'd miss that. Poor bastard.

"Aye, this fucker's hidden his glowing stronghold right out of everybody's sight!" Magnus said, clearly confused. He cracked his knuckles as he strobed bright and dull in the pulses from the tower. The snaps echoed deep into the pit below. "Who's gonna see it?"

"I don't know!" said Marigold. "Does the bastard want to be seen or not? Is he good with a spell, or is he shit? The arsehole did shake the mountain though, so I'm inclined to believe he's half decent at his craft, no matter how misguided it might be." He twizzled the short braid in his beard between forefinger and thumb, considering just who it might be that lay in wait for them. Didn't seem like any chanter he was aware of, though he couldn't discount the possibility that the specimen in question knew of him. "Well, whatever the story here is, we know where we need to go now."

"For the Will of the Worm!" yelled a chorus of unfamiliar voices from behind the group. Metal-clad feet hammered the rock and dirt as echoes of movement mingled with battle cries. A new wave of foes out of bloody nowhere just as Marigold and his men had locked themselves into a single-file trail.

"Cape-flapping cult shits," boomed Magnus.

Marigold twisted his feet on the narrow spit of path carefully, seeing four of the arse wipes hurtling along the path above. Each of them leapt up, as though the deathly fall below them simply didn't exist. All of them were plated in polished armour that gleamed blue in the strange light. Capes rippled in the humid air at their backs, while silver helmets made each appear identical. Now, Marigold had good hearing – he could shoot a man dead with a bow in a dense forest based on the snap of a twig alone – but these men must have been creeping behind them for some time to have got as close as they were now and he hadn't heard a thing. Marigold yanked the axe from its loop on his belt and hurled it at the group. Sailed right past each and every one of them and into the rock beyond. He bit off a curse as sparks fell and faded. He didn't *miss*. Never. Nothing about this bloody job was going well. Worst of all, this whole sorry scenario put Pettar right at the front of the proceedings, ready to endanger the whole crew and himself once again.

By fucking Greldin.

The lad reacted quickly, despite his ongoing sulking. He jerked his axe from his belt and embedded it deeply into the shoulder of the first man, between his iron pauldron and gleaming neck guard. It didn't gleam anymore. Still the neck, but Marigold had to admit the boy had at least switched it up from the knife. Maybe he had run out of knives. The sounds of tearing flesh and parting bone oozed into the upper reaches of the cavern, but the split cultist was engulfed in a crazed fury that held him strong beyond mortal blows. He smashed right into Pettar, flattening him against the rocky wall of the path, urging himself on to Marigold now that his time was very certainly limited. Haggar, the poor fucker, spun on the slender strip of rock in bewilderment as he tried to track all four of the bastards at once. Before Pettar could push himself back from the wall, the other three men – armed to the teeth and clad fit for a full-scale battle – barged past him again, apparently ignoring the youngster in favour of the four older men. That wasn't going to do Pettar's confidence any good. Whether they were actually right in the head or not, the cult members clearly understood where the danger lay. Sure-footed Haggar took the blow from the raging individual with finesse, but was still forced to abandon the giant axe on his back in favour gripping the cultist's trunk. Haggar launched the man up and snapped his bear-like palms around the fellow's thighs. With a tongueless cry, he swung the cultist like he was an axe himself. The three men behind him were thrust into the jagged rock wall by their sailing comrade. Sparks flew and metal dented. Snaps and wheezes told of broken bones and punctured lungs; plate armour was only good if it wasn't crushed. Haggar flexed his rippling arms and discarded his human weapon into the gaping chasm with ease. The doomed fucker's wail spread across the subterranean expanse, alerting anyone else down there to his horrific demise. Not that it really mattered; the opportunity for stealth had long since abandoned this quest. The three caped remainders halted their staggering for a moment as they heard the sharp slap and snap that signalled the end of their friend on the rocks far below.

Marigold, Magnus, and Ramage shifted impatiently from foot to foot on this single-file battlefield. Haggar was going to need help against the remaining three, but this line-up wasn't helping matters and Marigold didn't like it one damn bit. If a fight was happening, he wanted to be in it, not watching the fucking thing. Thank Greldin then that Pettar seemed to be taking this one more seriously than the last. There he was, ready to tackle the closest soldier, but just as his hands came down to grab him, a fifth cultist appeared out from the gloom and launched himself from the twist in the path above, landing iron-boot-first on Pettar's shoulders and slamming him face-first to the stone once again. Marigold only caught the briefest of glimpses of blood around his eyes and nose before Haggar's mass blocked the view.

With the enemy numbering four again, and all pushing forwards together, Haggar quickly lost his footing. The dumb bastard might be massive and incredibly strong but he was at a clear disadvantage in this fight. With a wordless bellow, Haggar whirled his arms as he fell backwards. Marigold could only watch impotently as his friend's eyes widened in the light from the throbbing tower. Haggar fell.

"Haggar!" yelled Magnus.

But Greldin was looking out for the man today. Haggar's hands slapped the smooth rock and gripped the ankle of the third cultist in the line. The deity clearly favoured him enough to keep him alive, even if he didn't care for his tongue.

"Fuck! Haggar, hang tight," cried Marigold. The Chief was now the next man in line to face the cult and that was exactly where he wanted to be. Marigold heard the tightening of a crossbow to his rear. Ramage. There was no time for Sear, no time to light her up. The Chief balled up his fist and smashed it into the jaw of the closest man. The blow set the man's face askew, knocking him out instantly. The poor bastard slumped to his knees and rolled sideways, tumbling over the edge of the pit. Miraculously – or unfortunately for him – the man's cape caught on the pointed rocks at the foot of the path, quickly trodden in by his struggling kinsman. The cape held fast, and the gurgling of a strangled throat bubbled up from below Marigold's feet. The click of Ramage's bow signalled the next move. "Mag, duck!" barked Marigold, and the two men dropped to a crouch.

Ramage fired his bow. The twang still shook in the air as the bolt struck deeply into the unarmoured slit over the groin of the next cultist. With accuracy like that, why in the Pits hadn't he aimed for an eye? Blood gushed forth like a river in a storm, black in the blue haze. Maybe he wasn't such a bad shot after all. The fluid flooded down the leg and onto the stone spit. It flowed beneath Haggar's arms, dripping over the edge. Haggar began to silently scramble at the slippery stone with the hand he didn't have around a cultist's leg. He was losing his grip.

Marigold sprang back up, Sear withdrawn in the motion. Her sharp edges would have to suffice on this occasion. He thrust his claymore forth in a brutal fashion, piercing metal and flesh and bone. Armour like that was no good against points, especially not points driven with the full fury of an enraged Marigold. Marigold clenched his substantial arms. Muscles writhed beneath his flesh as he wrenched his blade upwards, carrying the doomed man into the air with it. At the peak of the arc the cultist began to slide down the weapon. Before the still-alive bastard sunk too deep, Magnus tore him from the blade and cast him away to join his friend at the bottom, innards flapping wildly from the gash in the ruined man's side. Sometimes, having a friend even larger than himself came in very handy.

Two to go.

The next man was scrambling on the blood, trying to shake Haggar's grip from his ankle while Pettar was tightening the cape of the fellow at the back around his neck. Was the throat a fetish of his or something? Perhaps Elvi could reveal all. Still, the irony of the clothing choice was not to be missed: five men attacking, and already two had fallen foul to their own capes. Why wear the pissing things? Why give your enemy something to grab? The thought made Marigold pause for a moment as he considered the length of his braid down his neck and the beard on his chin. Not the same thing, and not the time for dwelling on his own fucking appearance while swinging Sear on a stretch of stone as wide as the blade itself. But he had mused long enough, for Marigold noticed too late the cultist's longsword rushing towards him. The cultist that had finally managed to free himself from Haggar's hands. Marigold shifted to one side, but not fast enough. The edge of the blade bit deeply into his left shoulder, through fur, through flesh, but thankfully not bone. The shock of the slice opened his hands immediately. Sear flew from his grip, clashing with the longsword and taking that with it. She twisted and gleamed in the blue light as she went over the edge with the dead ones.

"Fuck! My fucking sword!" Marigold roared. Even so, his right hand went to his shoulder. A finger deep. A bastard of a cut but not something that would stop him fighting. Hot blood coursed between his palm. He flicked his sodden hand to one side and booted his attacker savagely in the chest. "Ramage, next bolt! Fuck!" In a fit of rage, Marigold unslung Sear's sheath from his back and hurled it over the edge with her. He raged like a feral beast as the attacker stumbled back, clutching at his breastplate and gasping ragged breaths.

"I'm trying!" Ramage panicked.

The weaponless fucker between Marigold and Pettar's own little scuffle had nowhere to go.

Marigold could almost feel Magnus tensing behind him. There was no way Marigold could get out of the way to let the giant take over, and Haggar was now clinging to the edge of the drop with only the tips of his fingers. To risk another stabbing and rescue his friend, or tackle the cultist? Pettar already had one to deal with.

A loud snap came from the neck that Pettar was dealing with.

Just the one left then, and between the slits in that unarmed bastard's helmet, Marigold could see the eyes of a man aware that his final few moments were at hand. Hold on, Haggar. The nameless attacker let his bloodied sword clang to the stone, and hurtled forward, directly at Marigold. Did he think that would be quicker? Did he think he had a chance?

No.

The cultist leapt. He leapt so fucking high that it had to be some sort of party piece the coward had been honing his entire life. A deer would have been jealous of the height. The fellow's metal boot crunched onto Marigold's sliced shoulder, spurting blood from wound as the other foot punted Magnus in the cheek. Marigold bit back a growl as he twisted on the spot, catching sight of Magnus's fingers failing to grasp cultist or cape. The spring-heeled prick leapt over not only the man mountain, but Ramage on the other side as well. The local was *still* fucking fumbling with that bloody crossbow. Magnus was furious, helplessly stuck in the middle of it all. With Ramage still feverishly cranking the bow, Marigold turned back to check on Haggar only to find another shape rushing towards him. A grunt, another leap, and another foot used Marigold's shoulder as a stepping stone! Again! A sixth enemy? But there was no cape...

"I'll have the fucker, Chief!" A confident promise from overhead.

Pettar.

"I'll fucking have him and drag him back for you!" The lad, on a mission to impress it seemed, touched down on the stones of the path beyond the group.

"Eeeeeoooww!" came a strained voice from below.

Haggar!

"Fuck me, man, here." Marigold dropped to his chest and reached out. "Grab my arm, come on, man." Haggar's vice grip pulled painfully at the torn skin on Marigold's shoulder. Pettar's footsteps from beyond became a cacophony of echoes mixed with the enemy. "Ramage, Magnus, get after him!" Marigold ordered, lifting Haggar up onto the ledge. Was Ramage simple? What was he waiting for, blocking Magnus in like that? Marigold sometimes wondered if the men he surrounded himself with were even capable of thinking for themselves. You spend your life waiting for orders and it starts becoming difficult to do anything for yourself.

Letting the youngest of them run off like that... There were going to be roles set up when they were all out of this. Roles with responsibilities, roles that had his men having to decide shit for themselves. By Greldin, Marigold wasn't comfortable with the idea of telling his men to breathe in and breathe out, but it didn't feel like the day was far off.

The local and the goliath finally gave chase. Marigold plucked a discarded enemy sword from his feet, still slick with his own blood. It would have to do for now but it looked flimsier than wet firewood. Fuck. Marigold peered into the featureless abyss below, hoping for a glint of metal. He'd had Sear by his side for years, and she'd helped him out of certain death on more than one occasion. Where was he going to get another blade like that? The smith that made her was long dead. Marigold had made sure of it. He swung the substitute over the drop to clear the blood from it. He was sure the damn thing flexed even in the weak force of the air. Wouldn't even give it to a child to practice with. Didn't this *Crystal Cult* know a good blacksmith? Hadn't they stolen one from Elsdale? Arseholes.

A distant scuffle, a cry. Flesh hit hard ground somewhere further down the way.

"Oh fuck, no!" The voices were distant but clear. "Pettar! No! Ramage, grab him! You're alright, lad, you're alright. Oh fuck!"

Marigold felt prickly heat on his neck, tempered with a shiver along his arms. He gave Haggar the briefest of looks before the pair of them sped off along the tiny path, kicking up a cloud of grit and dirt. Haggar tore the axe from the fixing on his back and held it aloft, ready to slice in a heartbeat. The glow from the tower made the rock underfoot fuzzy, intangible, like it was contracting and expanding beneath their very feet. One slip and it was all going to be over. Had Pettar gone and slipped?

The track widened, arcing to their left as it hugged a wall overhung by dripping stalactites. The stones below were slippery, proper accident fuel. The tower took central stage in the great beyond, beating steadily like the very heart of the mountain. One of his men stood ahead, a silhouette within the luminescence of the tower. Hands alternating between hips and head. Despair. Marigold and Haggar closed in. The hitherto escaped cultist lay dead, face down on the damp path a few paces before his friends. A knife was wedged in his neck. Pettar's work, seemed he did have some blades left on him after all that had come before. Magnus was knelt by another downed figure while Ramage gestured helplessly at his side. It was Pettar. Pettar on his back, and there was *something* on top of him. Marigold's throat constricted as a thick nausea boiled in his belly. In the pulsing blue light, Marigold saw terror own Pettar's eyes. Marigold skidded down to his knees, the pain didn't register. Stones scattered over the edge. He shoved Magnus aside.

"By Greldin," Marigold gagged. "Just what in the fucking Pits is this?" he hissed to Magnus, Ramage, Haggar, anyone!

A black disc the size of a shitting shield stood vertically out of Pettar's chest. Several stubby black legs the length of Marigold's forearms wriggled delightedly along the sides. Eight of the things. The thing was solid, fat, and it seemed to be getting fatter before Marigold's very eyes. Some wretched demon or beast of the cult's was at work here. A vague sucking and clicking bubbled from within Pettar's chest. Pettar was trying to look anywhere but at the thing wedged in his torso. Blood leaked from the sides of his mouth, pooled on his chest around the point of entry. The lad was in agony. Petrified, and rightly so. Even Marigold felt the tingle of fear scraping the skin on his back.

"What happened?" Marigold asked Ramage and Magnus, not taking his eyes from Pettar.

"He... he... H-he just, he-"

"Pettar killed the shit that cut you," Magnus interrupted Ramage. "Saw him shove the knife right in. Good kill. Quick." Magnus spat, unable to take his eyes from Pettar. "Then this... this fucking *thing*, it burst out from the damn wall, fast as you like, bit right into his chest. Some fucking insect. Or something."

It was the biggest bastard insect Marigold had ever seen.

Marigold locked eyes with Pettar. "Well, lad," he said in the most soothing tone his gruff voice could manage, "you're going to have some impressive scars after this. Girls'll love 'em." He leaned back to survey the scene. "Magnus, Haggar, let's have it out, whatever it fucking is."

Pettar nodded slightly. Tears rolled, carrying streams of blood down his chin.

"Aye," Magnus agreed.

Haggar nodded solemnly.

"It's going to hurt, Pet, so you might want to bite down on this." Marigold tore an empty knife sheath from his belt and placed it between the lad's teeth. "Haggar, you hold his shoulders down, I'll steady his waist. Magnus, you good to pull?"

"Aye, Chief."

Magnus wrapped his huge arms around the weird creature and gripped tightly. It *hissed*.

"Ready? On three. One…" Marigold nodded almost imperceptibly at Magnus. "Two…"

Magnus heaved.

The screams from Pettar were unbearable. Marigold was more than used to the sound, but it was never easy to hear it coming from your own. A wet tearing, a sucking, a squelching. Pettar spasmed. A crack, a tear. Air rushed out, or was it in? Pettar's jaw slackened, the sheath flopped to the rock and stone. Magnus wrenched once more and stumbled back, clutching the black body of the beast between his tree-trunk arms and chest.

"Graaaargh!" He crushed it where he stood, drenching himself in the blood and innards of the monster.

"No, no, no, Marigold, the head!" cried Ramage, all but helpless in his flapping. "The head! It's still there, still inside!"

Marigold hung over the yawning wound as though it might consume him too. A round and black shape filled the space where he expected there to be flesh and bone. Blood flooded over the remnant of the creature that still appeared to be attempting to drink Pettar's life away. Up came the gore, a fountain that spurted out through the ragged hole that was the creature's severed throat. Marigold tore his furs from his back, frantically trying to staunch the flow. The material blackened. Soaked, useless. He cast it aside, thrust an arm out for another. Nothing materialised. He shook his open palm furiously, eyes glued to the vicious wound.

"Uh-uh," said Magnus.

Marigold breathed out, hurriedly glancing back and forth between Pettar's mutilated torso and face. The boy's eyes stared upwards into the cavern, unblinking, unmoving. Dead.

Silence fell over the remaining four as they slowly came to terms with the hideous result of the surprise battle. Ramage repeatedly pushed strings of sweat-soaked hair from his face, Magnus rammed his knuckles into his thigh. Haggar just sat down, cross-legged.

Marigold breathed deeply and spat his sigh out into the cavern. Back he threw himself, onto the cold, damp, and uncomfortable rock. He lay there, topless, covered in his blood, Pettar's blood, and the thick black mixture that had squirted from the creature. He turned his head sideways to stare at Pettar. Willed the chest to rise again. He hadn't brought the lad along to die. Sure, he could be infuriating, but the young ones always were. That's why they needed trips like this behind them, it was all part of growing up. Sweat soaked Marigold's back and front. Heat, fury, uncertainty, all washed over him in untamed waves. "Thought he could do with the experience," he said simply. "Wanted to toughen him up. Teach him how to be a man." And he knew it was his drunken decision that thought bringing him along would be a good idea. If he hadn't sobered up already, the last few seconds had truly sorted *that* out for him.

"No way you could have known, Boss," Magnus said quietly.

"He's dead, Magnus. Dead. Gone to fucking Greldin. He's just a lad. The Halls weren't made for lads."

"Died well, though, took out two of-"

"I just said he's dead, Magnus, for fuck's sake! Dying well is still dead. Dying well isn't going to somehow get him out of the reality that he is, in fact, dead. Is it?" Marigold snapped.

"No, Chief, but…".

"No, it's not." Marigold stopped and swallowed. He breathed deeply. "Let's just leave it at that. Fuck."

Of course, it *did* matter how Pettar had died, and Marigold knew it. If the lad had fallen over the edge of the trail it would have been a damn sight worse than meeting his end the way he did. He'd killed two of the cultists down here, and fucked up at least another two back in the church. Pettar was the first death in the clan since Marigold had been handed the reins, and they were reins he clearly didn't have the stones to handle properly. It hadn't taken long, all things considered. In many respects, he could have accepted the first death had it been Magnus or Haggar. Both men were seasoned warriors, and had under their belts a fine share of battle, of good times, of broken hearts. No death was a happy occasion, but at least they would have had stories behind them, tales to toast as their ghosts watched the world from high up in Greldin's Halls. There were no tales to tell for Pettar, save the one that saw him meet his grisly end. Elvi's little brother. Elvi's only family, that Marigold knew about.

Dead.

The first death of the clan under Marigold.

Not yet an adult.

Marigold closed Pettar's eyes and dragged the body away from the edge of the chasm. He sat him up against a cleft in the rock and the last of the blood in his chest poured out. "We can't take him down there with us, but we *will* collect him on our way back up. I'll carry him back myself." He stepped back from Pettar and kicked the crumpled carcass of the creature that had murdered him over the edge, into the blue gloom. "Just what in Greldin's name was that shitting thing?"

"Seemed to be some kind of gigantic tick, so it did," said Ramage, jerking about where he stood, like the mention of them set him off itching. "Looks just like the ones you get on livestock and wild animals, from what I can tell, know what I mean? By Fyr, though, what creature would something like that feed on to get so big?"

"Only something straight from the fucking Pits, Ramage, so you either cock that pissing crossbow now, or you chuck it over the ledge with the corpses and my fucking sword." Marigold jerked a thumb over his shoulder. "If there're more of them, they aren't going to wait for you to be ready to fire a shot. No wonder the cult are fully armoured. Best we use our smaller weapons from here. Pricks in robes, pricks with tens of legs, and a prick in the blue fucking tower. Any more pricks you know about around here, Ramage? Anything else we should watch out for down here? This Crystal Cult are going to wish they never set up shop in Spitertind."

Ramage readied his next bolt, muttering quietly.

Marigold took the lead, joined by Haggar and Ramage. Magnus remained with Pettar for a moment before slowly joining them. Marigold smeared the blood that leaked from the wound on his shoulder and growled like an annoyed bear. A matching scar for each side, and he had earned the previous one through a lack of fucking attention as well; wondering which part of a deer carcass to cut up first while some roughskin came at him with a knife. Fool. If he had paid more attention back there, would Pettar have even had the chance to leap over them? The boy would have been walking behind him right now if he'd just stabbed that bastard cultist in the eyes instead of worrying about his fucking braids.

"You hear that, Boss?" Magnus hissed as a chorus of male voices rose up the chasm.

"The cult has a choir. Why wouldn't it?" Marigold said flatly.

"They just sat waiting for us, having a sing-song?"

"We're only going to find out by going down, aren't we?"

"Right you are, Chief. Be good if they're all together."

It would be just fantastic in Marigold's book. Have them all primed to finish the barbarian intruders off before they made any more of a mess. Marigold was rarely one to dwell on his mistakes – the very few that he made – but the different choices he could have made in the last day were rushing around his head, yelling at him to be heard, as though that would change a thing. It was different being Chief. Death held more weight when the responsibility of it was his own.

The men trudged on in silence. Stones skittered on across the rough rock, over the edge. Drips hit shallow puddles and echoed back and forth. Sighs rose and fell. Heads were down, though eyes scoured the rock for anything round and black that might think about leaping out at them.

The Cerulean Hair became thicker and brighter on the uneven walls as the path snaked down into the belly of the mountain. This crystal keep, the focal point of the mountain interior, rippled alternating shades of blue, drawing closer with every step but still appearing an impossible distance away. The bottom of this hell hole seemed to be flat, lighter, perhaps even sandy. The tower sat some distance away in this deeper realm. Black stalagmites reached up around the tower's foundations and peppered the lower levels of the cave around it, some were almost half as high as the bastard tower itself. The Chief, the Giant, the Mute, and the Local each clutched their remaining weapons as they pressed on into the heart of the mountain. It sounded like the setup for some shit joke.

"With luck, that'll be the first and last surprise. With even more luck, there'll be something dead beneath my feet by the end of the day."

Marigold spat. A shit joke with a shit punchline.

Chapter Five

HIT THE ROOF

The chanting stopped the moment Marigold set foot on the sandy base of inner Spitertind. Where were the bastards? The Chief peered carefully over the lip of a roughly hewn hole in a carved wall that continued on from the path. Smoothed to just over the height of a man, it resembled a more standard rock face from there on upwards: cracked, irregular, natural. He held a hand close to his chest, wary of any further surprise attacks from oversized insects. A small cavern lay beyond the hole. Balls of Cerulean Hair were clumped together here and there, rudimentary lanterns that revealed basic chairs, tubular carvings of stone, and an uncomfortable looking bed frame of moulding wood. Hard, flat, nothing soft to rest a head on. Then again, these cults often loved a spot of self-flagellation. Marigold had no idea why. "Guess we know where the cult hides their numbers, then," he said, pushing himself away from the wall as he eyeballed countless identical holes and openings that continued along it and stretched around the entirety of the base of the mountain. Hundreds of the fuckers, if there was one for each hollow. Thousands if they had to share.

"Nobody home?" asked Magnus.

"Not here," replied Marigold, sullenly.

"Shame," said Magnus, sounding genuinely upset as he cracked his knuckles once more. "Shall we try the next?"

"If you want."

The group huddled closely in the sandy expanse. The chorus might have stopped, but at no point during the twisting descent had Marigold been able to determine the source. Marigold looked up into the hazy blue to see the high shelf they left Pettar's body on. They'd be back for him. No way one of Marigold's men was going to remain in some pissing cave, no matter how irritating the little cunt had been at times. He was one of the clan. Marigold gritted his teeth: Pettar's death was not the first conversation he wanted to have upon his return to the group, but he couldn't see a way that it could be avoided. How in the Pits was he going to explain Pettar's death to Elvi? Marigold bit hard on the inside of his lip as he tried not to go over the last moments of the lad. Why was he dwelling? Because Pettar's death would irrevocably change things with the woman of his desires? Was he sad for Pettar or himself?

The vast and shimmering tower stood before them, claiming the centre of this grand chamber. The thing looked like a colossal strut, a pillar that held up the mountain. Who knew? Perhaps now that the fucking place had been hollowed out the tower *was* the only thing keeping it up?

Magnus strode ahead across the soft, blue-tinged sand. Marigold let the others follow him. Haggar held his twin-bladed axe ahead, clearly not taking any more chances by leaving it strapped to his back. To Ramage's credit, his crossbow – wound and ready to go – had been stowed in favour of a basic, woodcutting axe. Wood, limbs, necks. The axe wouldn't give a shit what it was fed.

This underworld was a curious land to behold: the sand, the smooth sections of the rock, the holes. It was almost as though the very mountain itself had been melted from the inside. In an attempt to occupy himself with something other than death, Marigold began to count the cavities that might or might not hide the rest of this elusive cult. The weird, murky light made telling rock from hole somewhat difficult and he gave up at thirty. Still, even that would already be enough to overwhelm them if they emptied and mounted a surprise attack. There could be hundreds of the fucking Crystal Cult members living here in the darkness, like worms. And, Marigold mused, there had to have been hundreds at one point; carving out the inside of a bloody mountain wasn't going to have been a quick or easy task, and he had to admit that they'd made a fairly good job of it. How long had they been here? The Crystal Cult had allegedly been stealing men, women, and children from Elsdale for longer than that uptight barkeep could remember, so the story had been told. It had to have taken years for this sect of madmen to get the mountain into the state it was in, and to what end? To hide a pissing tower? Is that what the townsfolk were for? Hard labour? Marigold looked around, across the expanse of light sand, up the black rock walls and tower to the infestation of vicious stalactites that soared overhead. They had to have been worked to dust if that was the case, there wasn't sight nor sound of a single one. A warm drop of liquid landed on his cheek as he stared up. It tasted metallic. Marigold snorted. Magic shook the mountain earlier, and magic could just have easily hollowed it out with or without the missing folk.

Magnus turned ahead and called to Marigold. They were some distance out already. Marigold gestured irritably and reluctantly jogged to join them. Each footfall felt like it tore his shoulder apart just a little more, and he no longer cared about chewing off the odd growl or curse: he supposed there was little point in maintaining any form of silence now. Between the bell above and the scrap on the cliff, every cult member remaining undoubtedly knew that intruders were afoot. If only the moss bloomed brighter. The light was welcome, but the shadows along the edges were unnerving, even for Marigold. As the tower continued to pulse slowly, he tried to pierce the impossible depths. Nothing waiting, it *seemed*. Maybe each and every one of the fuckers had holed themselves up in that tower.

Time to find out.

Each man paced purposefully across the sand, crunching it underfoot and splashing tiny puddles as they closed in on the tower. To kill cultists, avenge Pettar, and to save Elsdale. The vast structure had appeared massive from the twisting paths above, yet down here it seemed even grander.

"Now, just how would a man go about making all this?" Ramage pondered aloud.

"Fuck knows," said Magnus.

"Oh, I know," said Marigold, fairly sure of himself. "Magic, magic, pissing magic. You know, these wizard cunts spend their whole, misguided lives trying to master one form of spell or the other? Sometimes they get good at them. And if it's not a wizard? Well, there's only one other creature I know able to create towers like that, though I've neither seen one nor found anything so big made by them in years."

"What's that then, Chief?" Magnus asked.

Ramage drew breath sharply, recoiling from nothing that Marigold could see. "A... A Ta- You dinnae think there's a Tall Man down here, d'you?" he gasped, voice clipping as he guessed at the name of the beast Marigold had suggested. You could practically hear the sweat forcing its way out.

"Well, probably not," said Marigold. "Think we'd have met it by now if there was one, or at least heard or seen it. They don't fear men, don't hide from them. Actively seek them out, really."

Ramage made an exasperated noise.

"Never seen anything made of such a material. Doesn't look to be stone. Tall Men use stone, they are geomancers, after all."

"Then why in the Pits are you bringing the name up?" Ramage squeaked.

"To keep you all on your toes," Marigold said plainly, noting the genuine fear there. Ramage seemed safe enough for now.

"S'pose it's made of crystal, Chief. Crystal Cult 'n' all that."

"S'pose you're right, Mag," said Marigold. "Doesn't look like there's much in the way of crystal elsewhere down here though."

Haggar traipsed alongside Marigold with his head down, dragging the blade of his axe in the sand. Poor bastard just wanted to join in on the conversation.

Marigold's neck ached, continually craning it see the top of the tower as he was. The closer he got, the further back he bent. He found his eyes following the mesmerising ripples of light that began at the bottom and slid slowly upwards. What in the name of Greldin was that? It almost seemed alive, which was ridiculous. Some kind of sorcerous shield? What would happen if he touched it? Would he burst into flame? Drop dead? Have his stones shrivel up and drop off? It was quite easily the single-most odd construction that Marigold had ever seen, and he had seen a lot of weird shit in his years of butchering wizards, witches, warlocks, druids, alchemists, illusionists, conjurors, necromancers... If Greldin was smiling upon them all today, maybe he'd find some new type of spell-meddling fuckwit to add to that list, if such a man or woman or beast even existed.

"Don't see a way in, Chief," Magnus said, gripping his knuckles yet again. The snaps rushed out into the blue-black depths. How the man managed to crack his digits so often was one of life's great, unanswered questions.

"Well, there has to be a way in somewhere, doesn't there?" Marigold answered back. Of course there would be a way in; Marigold doubted the sanity of spellcasters, not their intelligence.

"I'm sure there is, Chief, but I don't see it. Better not be back at the fucking top. Shit, Chief, you think we were meant to go in from the top of the mountain? What if we came in the wrong way?"

"Then we've another bloody climb on our hands. Let's just take a look around the back of the bastard first, eh? Before we make any rash decisions."

Marigold led the way. Hopping over meandering streams that cut shallow ridges into the sand. The water seemed to be rushing down the tower itself, now that they were closer. The sides glistened in the ethereal light. The streams spread out in all directions from the base of the tower, like the wriggling legs of some vast spider. The rivulets ate deeper into the powdery floor the further they stretched from the tower. Deep pools of water began to dot this bizarre underworld, reflecting the azure light, rippling gently when drops from above landed in them and casting the illusion of even greater depth further below. The enormous cavern was filled with the padding of clomping boots and the bass beating of the magic that coursed through the infernal tower.

Round and round they went, nothing revealed itself. Not a door, a window, not even a shitting crack.

"Maybe you're fucking right, Magnus, Greldin's teeth! There's no way in down here, at least nothing we'll get through without knowing the damn spell that opens it." The Chief hurled the inferior longsword he had scavenged point-first into the sand and ground a fist into his palm. "Fuck it, let's just go back up. Ramage, I know how this looks, but these are strange circumstances. For what it's worth, I expected the whole sum of them to be waiting at the top, this shitting world of something else was entirely unexpected."

"Don't you worry about that, Marigold," Ramage chirped, waggling a finger at the air as he slipped his axe back into the loop on his belt. "You've shown me these bastards can be beaten, so you have. Whether we cross blades with them today or tomorrow, I'm already feeling better about the future, so I am."

"I'm not worried, Ramage. We're still going to put an end to these bastards…" Marigold confirmed.

Magnus and Haggar sighed with relief, grinning at one another.

"…And we're doing it today. If we don't get in at the top, we'll find another way. And if we need another way, we'll bring along a host of warriors from the clan. There're more than a few that are going to want to deal out some retribution on Pettar's behalf."

"Back the way we came, then?" Ramage sighed.

"Looks like it."

The four men turned on the spot and began tracing the line of their footprints and the grooves from Haggar's axe head back across the sand and around the enormous, curving wall of the glowing tower. Marigold grumbled to himself with each step. It wasn't the first time he'd met with disappointment, but most of this trip had become one large disappointment and he was the one making the plans. It just so happened to be his first real job in the role, too. Victory had seemed to come easy in previous ventures, back when the stakes weren't resting on his shoulders. He looked back at the tower, willing a door to appear. At least he hadn't brought the whole clan with him for this. His companions were oddly quiet all of sudden. Haggar tapped a firm finger on Marigold's arm and pointed ahead.

"Oh Fyr..." whispered Ramage.

Before the men stood a vast assemblage of cultists arranged in a wide arc that barred the way between the ensorcelled tower and the rocky path back up. This was no group ripe for a small skirmish; it seemed to Marigold that every last bastard in this Pit-spawned cult stood before them and whatever form of freedom lay on the other side. Each of them wore the same; plate boots, greaves, chest piece, and helm. The now familiar blue cape hung from every neck. Hard to tell which were men and which were women, any individuality lost in the uniform of the cult. Within the middle of the congregation was a large, black mass just back from the front row. Was it fabric? Something covered? An idol? A weapon? A beast? Whatever it was, it was almost twice the height of the men around it, and it hadn't been sat in that spot earlier. Fuck, was there really a Tall Man here? Whatever fight was about to kick off, it wasn't going to go well for the intruders if they had to start fighting one of those particular monsters. What was that about not bringing the whole clan?

The gathering began to shuffle carefully around the group, moulding the arc into a circle. Easily a hundred of the bastards against four, but still they showed caution. That cheered Marigold up a little, even if the force was so great that those further away appeared hazy in the blue gloom. This had to be the army of which Ramage spoke, and to be fair, it *was* some host. Perhaps they really should have checked each window in the walls. Still, Marigold had fought his way out of worse, and with fewer men at his back. Even so, he hadn't been trapped in an unknown cavern on any of those previous occasions. Time to look at the positives. Here was blood to spill, bones to snap, flesh to rend: the barbarian's delight. A cull was imminent. The Crystal Cult's ranks were about to meet a long-overdue thinning. Marigold's hand instinctively went for Sear. Fuck. Tooth and nail it was, then. He would rip the throat from as many of the cunts as he could.

"Finally, a decent fight," Magnus chuckled.

"You ready?" Marigold asked, chiefly addressing Haggar and Magnus.

"Aye," said Magnus, popping knuckles once again.

Haggar remained silent.

The caped men at the front of the line drew their weapons, and the same sounds behind told of the whole circle following suit.

"Let's see to it that our loss wasn't for nothing." Marigold stepped ahead of his own men. "Let's see to it that this Crystal Cult fear a barbarian when they see one. Give 'em no quarter, tear 'em limb from fucking limb." The Chief began a slow trot towards the men, breaking into a run. His heart pounded, as it did before any fight. Anticipation, fury, blood lust. There was no fear. He screamed the ragged roar of a feral beast. No words, just rage. Teeth bared, spit frothed, eyes widened. The coating of his own blood spattering his neck and face likely completed the effect of a berserker utterly lost in the rush of the fight. He clenched the muscles in his thick arms, an arc of death ready to grab the first unfortunate bastard they could reach. And they were powerful arms, the recipient would not be fighting back. In a scrap, Marigold was more animal than man. Haggar and Magnus started behind him, pounding the soft sand like a war drum. The cultists at the inner edge of the circle edged back nervously, murmuring oaths, readying weapons and stances. The sight of a mere three barbarians hurtling towards hundreds still rattled them.

Something moved from the within the crowd. The dark shape. A cloth fell. Flesh appeared.

No use getting disheartened now. Marigold thrust his shoulders forward, head down, fingers clawing the air. His lungs emptied their scream as his first punch smashed the jaw of an unshaven chin below a helmet.

"Strike," a calm voice commanded. It was somewhere within the cult mass.

Thud, thud, thud.

Blinding light spewed into Marigold's vision. *What?* His right cheek was intense pressure. Heat. His neck felt like it might snap right there and then, if it hadn't done so already. His momentum was slain as he found himself stumbling back, bewildered.

"Again." That same voice.

A blurry, white mass swung in front of him, and his left cheek felt much like the right.

Marigold slammed nose first into the damp sand. He snorted as he tried to push himself up. Blood caked his face, sand clung to his skin. His arms sagged. Marigold dropped back into the mushy ground. What the fuck?

"All of them, then! Come on, boy, hop to it."

Marigold heard several other dull slaps by his sides. With some difficulty, Marigold twisted his throbbing neck to see Magnus eating the dirt, same as him. To his left, Haggar was trying to force himself back up. Ramage's uneasy steps padded the sand behind. No doubt the man was wondering whether testing his luck now was really a viable option. Three barbarians felled within the blink of an eye. What a fucking disaster this trip was. Jeering laughs flooded the air. A chorus of sniggers mocked the barbarians as they strained to understand the circumstances that had brought them to their bellies.

Thud, thud, thud.

It was time to find out.

Marigold's neck cracked painfully as he forced himself to look ahead. Two feet encased in beaten plate metal, larger than any feet he had seen before – and Marigold himself wasn't lacking – were planted firmly in the sand. The chief pushed himself onto his knees, wiped a forearm across his bloodied, sandy face. His beard was already crispy and matted with blood and grit. He traced the feet over thick, tree-trunk legs that were covered by a cut of brown sack cloth from the knee upward. Skin the colour he'd expect of a man. A man did this? Marigold could take down a bear with nothing more than the hands Greldin gave him. What kind of monstrous *man* could smash the storied barbarian to the ground like this? Or Magnus? Marigold couldn't remember any time when Magnus had been floored by a fist, and he was fairly sure that it wasn't because of a developing concussion. His head spun, the ground became the walls, the walls the ceiling. Nausea washed over him but he couldn't afford to pass out here. He mastered the chaos that swilled within his skull. As his head twisted involuntarily, he saw the legs become thighs. Fists like great joints of ham swung lazily by the creature's side, blood dripped from the knuckles. Just two fists though, so it really wasn't a Tall Man. The torso continued the giant frame. Thick, iron chains hung from shoulders and wound around the slab this thing called a waist. Marigold's neck hurt like a bastard but he craned back far enough to see the face of this monster. The head looked on at nothing in particular, utterly ignorant of his foes below. Bulging, brown eyes seemed to stare off in different directions, divided by greasy strips of black hair. A look of utter idiocy painted the face. The fucking prick *was* a man, though. A giant man, and quite possibly a simple one.

"Bravo," came a gentle voice to the side of the titan. "Cease, my son." There was that commanding tone again.

A sigh of obvious relief came from Ramage, who had no doubt been pissing himself at the prospect of taking those knuckles to his face. Rightly so, Marigold had to admit between the pulses of pain his jaw.

Against his best efforts, the Chief fell back to the sand while he attempted to locate the source of the new voice. He stumbled back to his kneeling position, but it was too late to save face now. He brushed the sand from the hairs at the top of his bare chest. Caked in blood. His blood. That gash in his shoulder was full of dirt and sand. Marigold glared ahead. An old man, barely half the size of the giant, stood by its side. The ancient fellow softly clapped his hands together with a wet patting, a look of delight painted a lined face, framed by a white beard, short and neat. If Marigold hadn't been knelt before the bastard with blood leaking from his nose and mouth, he might have said the fucker even looked kindly. It was something in those soft, tired eyes. This old cultist's head was completed by a tall, pale blue headdress that looked like it would fall off if the man did anything other than shuffle along. Gold hemmed and dotted with bright blue stones, it featured a blue strip running up the centre that had to be an approximation of that fucking tower behind them. Obsession: the definition of a cult. White and blue robes with a gold trim hung from his slight frame. The robe seemed to cover the elderly man's body entirely. A long staff – as tall as the fellow himself – was held within the crook of his elbow; a plain white shaft with a blue-jewelled top. Blue, blue, and more fucking blue. Marigold was going to have to rethink his favourite colour. Green. Green from now on. He spat blood into the sand with the force of a bolt. Carefully, he tested his knees and began to push himself up to a crouch and closed his eyes to master the dizziness. "So, you're the prize prick, eh? The leader down here?" His voice was still strong, at least.

"You could say I'm the, er… head, of our little congregation, yes," the old man agreed with a grin.

"That your wand, then?" He gestured to the staff. "Big isn't it? Very impressive. Big tower, big mountain, big lackeys, big staff. Size matters for you, doesn't it?" It seemed about the perfect time to bring out the manhood quips; if he managed nothing else before he was killed, at least he could piss the bastards off.

The crowd of men surrounding them shuffled their feet. Impatient. They wanted blood. He'd pissed *some* of them off, at least.

Marigold squinted at the old git, still swaying a little. "Of course you're the shit in charge. It's hardly going to be this fucking simpleton, is it?" He cast an open palm in the direction of the lummox. "By Greldin's fucking axe, I thought I could count all of the men bigger than me on one finger," he said. "Suppose I'll need two for the time being, while this cunt still breathes."

"He's huge," Magnus grumbled.

"Fucking massive," Marigold agreed.

Haggar made some sort of agreeable groan from the other side as blood from his mouth pattered softly to the sand.

"Must be half man, half giant, half-fucking-bear," Magnus continued.

"That's three halves, you idiot," Marigold sighed. Would today's embarrassments ever end?

"Probably explains why he's that big, so it does" Ramage hissed from the back of the group.

"Still there, are you?" Marigold muttered.

"Oh, he is large, isn't he?" the man in the headdress said, gazing reverently at the giant. "The Roof is our pride and joy among us."

"The Roof?" snorted Marigold. By Greldin, what kind of a stupid bloody name was that?

"Yes, The Roof," the elderly man confirmed. "Oh, I see that look of disdain in your eyes, but in time you'll come to revere him too. The Roof is tall. The Roof is strong. The Roof completes what our mundane muscles cannot. For all of that, we are most grateful. The Roof is the proof of what man can become when they choose the right path of worship."

The Roof, whatever he damn well was, remained blissfully ignorant of the men that held him in such high regard. Marigold tried and failed in his search for a hint of intelligence in that face. "Well," he began, "your *Roof* seems to be watching the cavern in two directions at once. That a specific skill of his?"

"You mock us," the old man said, laughing curtly. He was too softly spoken, like some frail grandparent, or a man that wanted something but knew that the force he possessed wasn't enough to attain it. Odd for a wizard; they usually seemed so sure of themselves. "The Roof needs only my instruction. His mind doesn't need to be filled with the worries and thoughts of men such as you or I. The Roof is power, The Roof is strength. We think for him, we guide him along the right path."

"So, he *is* simple!" Marigold concluded, finally pushing himself up to standing straight. His dark surroundings twisted around him, but he steeled himself and planted his feet firmly in place.

"Hmm, men tend to stay down once The Roof has been at them" mumbled the old man. A grimace developed on his face. "Most curious."

"Well, friend, we aren't most men," Marigold said, spitting another glob of bloodied saliva into the sand between himself and the row of cultists. The insides of his lips were shredded. "You'll find out soon enough." Antagonising the enemy in this situation was probably as poor an idea as coming here with a handful of men in the first place was. Had The Roof punched him 'simple' as well?

"Indeed. I wonder, friends, did you happen to encounter one of our number on your journey here? A man named Russel?"

"Aye, we did." Marigold said, over a loud gulp from Ramage. "Ran into him back in Elsdale, and I've no doubt his corpse is still there. You've him to thank for us being here."

Murmurs of anger and surprise bubbled out through the cult. Feet came forwards.

"Can't allow this!"
"The Lord won't be pleased!"
"Lord? What about Cecil?"

"Look, look, calm! Allow me to start this all over again," the cultist's spokesman said, stepping back. "Allow me to introduce myself properly: I am Lennan, the High Priest of this particular sect of the Crystal Order. Why is it that you are here, disturbing us? Who might you fellows be? What are your names?" Lennan began to wring his hands together, clearly he was becoming impatient with the situation.

"Rama-"

"Don't say a fucking word, woodcutter" Marigold interrupted. "They're going to kill us no matter what."

Ramage swallowed loudly again.

"Now, now, I certainly won't be killing any of you," Lennan said.

"Of course you won't be, you old cunt," Magnus said, hurling his own gift of bloodied spit at The Roof's feet. "This bastard here's the one that'll be snapping our necks."

"Come on, let's try to defuse this situation," Lennan laughed gently. "We do prefer our prisoners to be alive for when we need them. Dead flesh is so... well, dead!" Lennan chuckled a stupid little giggle. Perhaps senility was well-established in the old coot.

"Feast! Feast! Feast!" chanted the crowd behind the The Roof and Lennan.

"Very reassuring," Marigold deadpanned. The cult were cannibals? Is that where everyone was? Foaming in bellies and resting in big piles of shit? "So," he asked calmly. "How many do you reckon we can take down before this big bastard here puts us down? Lennan here says he won't kill us, so the stakes have been reduced somewhat. What do you think? Ten? Twenty? More? Think if we just twist this old prick's head from his neck the rest'll scatter?"

"Worth a try, Chief," Magnus said steadily.

Haggar grunted in confirmation.

"Crossbow's ready," said Ramage, though he did not sound convinced.

"Right then." Marigold flexed his arms, swung his mostly unwound braid behind his neck and squeezed the blood from his beard. He took a step forward, less steady than he had hoped he would be, but he continued with his other foot regardless. "Come on, then, you caped fucking arselickers!"

"Strike, now!" Lennan's voice was panicked.

The Roof was big, but The Roof only had two eyes, and apparently Marigold was stood in The Roof's rather large blind spot. The chief ducked below bough-like arms, beneath glistening leg muscles that coiled and writhed like scrapping snakes under the skin. Marigold rushed the crowd. Lennan stumbled backwards as the cultists admitted him into relative safety. Marigold forced himself between wobbling swords that lacked both conviction and solid craftsmanship; the bastards clearly hadn't expected they would need to use them with their precious Roof on hand. A 'crack' and a 'thunk', Marigold snatched a glimpse of Haggar already hitting the deck. Marigold felt slices along his arms as he forced himself in deep, but cuts weren't going to drop him now. The circle tightened. No escape, but the cultists were offering themselves up. One neck snapped. Two. Three. Arms bent back at the elbow, collarbones crumpled, blood fled from lips. A bellow that came from lungs greater than his called out from behind. Flesh slapped flesh and Magnus was hurled overhead into the crowd, still clutching a cultist he held by the throat. A line of capes crumpled beneath the human missile. Magnus would have loved to have been conscious for that. Marigold's fist bore so deeply into the stomach of the man before him that the breastplate dented. Blood fountained from the victim's mouth and nose. Something sliced his leg, still nothing vital. Ramage cried out, silenced almost immediately amidst the stomping of hulking feet. Just the Chief left, now. It wasn't uncommon for Marigold to be the last man standing in a fight, but this one was fast becoming bleaker than most. The cultists surrounded him. Blows struck him from the left and right, but still he fought, roaring at the top of his lungs. Everything blurred around him, helmeted heads bled into one another, knees lost themselves in dark recesses of flesh. Cultists were falling all around. How many had he dropped? He hadn't a clue.

Then they stopped. The circle opened up around Marigold.

Marigold didn't need to see what was happening to know what was coming.

"Do it! Now!" shrieked Lennan's feeble voice from within the crowd.

Was Marigold going to be able to get his hands on that devout fucker before The Roof laid hands on him?

No.

Marigold felt hot and clammy palms grip his shoulders. The ground disappeared from beneath his feet. A blurred vision of flesh and loincloth and solidity took him. A brief moment of freefall ended as he ploughed spine-first into the sand, creating a Marigold-shaped crater that he struggled to pull himself out of. Marigold had a split-second to see The Roof's obscene frame lumbering towards him. The air hissed. Stars swam in his eyes before he even realised he had felt the blow. The next one struck him in the solar plexus. He held back the vomit and crashed to his knees once again. He never got another chance to look his foe in at least one of his eyes before a granite fist bore down into the back of his head.

Chapter Six

THE BIRTH SEA SISTREN

Stars twinkled on the edges of Marigold's vision as he came to. What had he been drinking? His face felt like a roughskin had been using it as stress relief. Drool and blood hung in strings from his puffy lips. Sand rolled by below. He felt his feet carving a small ravine in the ground. He was being dragged, fingernails dug into the soft flesh of his armpits. The passage he was being pulled through was dim, torchlit in a miserly fashion. Marigold blinked. His right eye hurt more than his left. Felt heavy. Felt fat. Instinctively, he tried to paw at it. Both hands moved together. Bound. Chains. Of course he was tied up. He was lighter too, relieved of the meagre weaponry he knew he'd had on him. Why had he let that happen? He let his head hang down so he could see his waist. Sear's vial remained tucked away just behind his belt, out of sight. Abruptly, he remembered the The Roof, remembered the fists. A ringing broke into Marigold's ears. Voices began to eat through.

"Should've just killed them there and then," a nasal voice complained from above. "Look at the size of them! Did you see the eyes on this bastard? He's an animal! Any chance to let *him* breathe again is another chance for us to all die for it."

"Pah! They're chained up tight, look!" An older voice replied. Marigold barely felt the shakes the man made. "And besides, you know Lennan likes to see them alive when our Lord takes them up inside."

Taken up inside?

"Yeah, but does it really matter?" said Stuffed Nose. "Food's food, and he'll be ready to leave soon. Do you think he cares whether his meals wriggle or not?"

"Stop fretting, Hugo, they're not going to cause us any more trouble, and our Lord doesn't relish dead meat, you should know *that* by now."

"Won't cause trouble? Everyone causes trouble! Elsdale folk're weak, but not these. What makes you think they'll just go with what we ask?"

"Like I just said, they're bloody chained up. And they'll stay that way 'til Lennan's ready for them. I don't care how strong they think they are, they're not breaking out of these chains or the cells we're dragging them to. And just say something did happen, against all the odds? The Roof'll see to it, just how he saw to them before. They'll be at the Table soon, and then the job's done."

The Table? That was very obviously a name in Marigold's mind. Who in the Pits was this Table character? A brother of The Roof? By fucking Greldin, was he going to have to face The Chair and The Door before breaking out of this place? Who was in charge of the names around here?

"If you say so, Ture. What about their friends outside? The ones outside the town, I mean. You don't just get one or two barbarians, they're like rabbits, fucking their sisters, their mothers, their daughters. Hundreds of the bastards and they're all perpetually wound up on account of the inbreeding, all gagging for their next fight. They're a fucking plague, wherever they go. What happens when they realise their comrades are missing? Hmm, Ture?

"I don't know, Hugo, what's going to happen?"

"They're all going to be piling inside here, that's what! What are we going to do when they cut us down?

Cut our Lord down? All of our hard work undone, and all because we insist on-"

"Ugh! Hugo, will you just shut up? We're nearly done here, our Lord is almost ready to leave, He is the greatest there ever was and His size is all thanks to our love for Him. Once He moves on we'll move on to the next one, within the month Lennan says – though I doubt we'll find such a grand Lord again. Far north, I heard, northern coasts of Rosaria. Nobody's going to follow us that far for a few dead men, just give it a bloody rest. Elsdale mounted any rescue attempts yet? No, not in two generations. We've had nearly all of them by now, and we'll finish off any stragglers before we go."

Marigold carefully glanced around, hoping it just seemed like his head was swinging. The walls were close, he couldn't see how high. Some narrow cave or ravine, and it had been some bloody effort just to discover that. He let his head sink back down. His whole body ached. Ached more than it had after any beating in recent memory. That Roof was a tough one, no matter how fucking ridiculous his name was. Involuntarily, he twitched at a spasm of pain deep in his lower back. His chains clinked and jangled.

"Oh look, Hugo, your favourite one's awake."

"Well knock him back out! Fuck me, Ture, what if he-"

"Quiet, both of you. Those chains will hold him just fine," an old and dusty voice hissed. "They'll hold them all just fine. Stop panicking and get them to the cells. The sooner they're safely locked up the sooner we can find out where the rest of them are hiding, and the sooner our Lord can be served the meal He so deserves. A fine meal indeed."

Lennan. Old bastard. Marigold tested his arms and sighed. That shithead was on borrowed time. It was all a matter of biding his own.

Groans and more jangling broke out from behind him. At least one of his friends was still alive.

"Fuck me, my fucking head. What did we drink?"

"Knuckles," Marigold croaked at Magnus.

"Ah, yeah."

New sets of footsteps joined, coming from ahead. A new group coming towards them.

"Cluny!" Ramage's pained voice broke out from somewhere behind Marigold.

Marigold forced his head up again to see a bloodied and defeated-looking man being dragged along by the arms. The cultists either side were without helmets. Both held a look of grim determination on their faces, and both were remarkably young. Probably younger than Pettar was. Had been. The man, Cluny, drooled as he stared at the sand pass beneath him.

"Cluny, what have they done to you?" Ramage wailed.

The eyes on this Cluny shifted up to gaze at Marigold's line, though his head remained hanging. As the two groups passed one another, Marigold noted the crooked angle of Cluny's legs: clearly shattered. The man must have been in agony, but whatever else they'd done or said to him was far worse than the physical pain he was so clearly in. Cluny's eyes dropped back to the floor.

"Oh no, no, no no. That's us, so it is, it is it-"

A sharp slap silenced Ramage.

"Take him to the entrance, but hold him there till I return," Lennan's voice rasped at Marigold's rear left. "It won't be long now, and I *must* be there when it begins. I shan't miss the final meal, and it will be soon, mark my words."

"Yes sir," barked the two men in unison. "Er, sir?"

"Hmm, yes?"

"What if it's the last? What if the Lord don't need these fellas?"

"Well we'll just leave them locked up, or else let The Roof play with them." Lennan chuckled quietly.

The pathway narrowed as it delved deeper into the mountain's foundations, the procession of cultists organised themselves into single-file. A knee bashed into Marigold's swollen eye. The Chief snarled and shot a glare at the perpetrator, fuck the pain in his neck he wanted to know which particular bastard was responsible for that. Black beard, over-sized nose, rippling jowls. Congratulations to him, he was now a marked man.

The others ahead began to slow down as a jarring scrape of rusted metal on rusted metal screeched around the small space. A row of cells had been built into the end of the tunnel, and from the state of the metalwork on them, were clearly some of the earlier additions to this underground hideout. Uncomfortable looking bastards they were; low and with jagged ceilings, walls glistening with algae in the firelight, small black rocks jutted up from the sand on the ground. A real home from home.

"Here we are, your new lodgings for the time being. Come on, men, let's have them in there." Lennan actually sounded proud to be offering such dire accommodation.

Marigold was dragged to his feet by six arms. Weak whoresons! Wasn't there a man here among them? Marigold was at least able to confirm that the space was too small and tight for The Roof to have joined them. He was shoved with some force into the dank space, almost tripped as his chains tightened behind him. A disgruntled grumble joined the clinking of slack chains. Groggily, Marigold found Haggar shaking his head by his side. Magnus was pushed inside, then Ramage. No sharp weapons, the only metals on them were chains and belt buckles. That vial of Sear's fluid might have some use yet, Greldin knew it wasn't going to slide into her hilt anymore. He still couldn't believe he'd lost her, not after all these years. He hoped the man that found it stabbed himself in the foot with it or swung it through his own bastard neck. Magnus stalked the front of the cage with a grimace that Marigold would normally have expected to be capable of cutting steel. But, as all four of them remained linked together it seemed that wasn't to be the case today. One of the cultists slotted their torch into a metal fixture that jutted from the rocky wall outside the cell. The cell door clanged shut. A chain rattled as it was wound around the exit.

"We may have imprisoned you for the time being…"

Marigold lurched in the direction of the elderly voice and glowered at the source through strings of bloodied hair. Truth be told, he felt like passing out again from the effort.

"My, you are a mess. Still, glare all you like, my friend. Nothing will change, but, er… where was I? Ah, yes! Light! We shan't deny you light. This cell isn't exactly a comforting one, but there are worse. Ask your new friend, Nina. Now, I'm sure you'll understand why we've locked you up in here, invading us and killing us."

"Fuck you, Lennan," Marigold replied. "How about you remove the chains and open the door? Discuss this like men."

"I rather think that men discuss matters with words, not violence. Besides, the time for unchaining will come. You shan't be here forever," the elderly man said in his kindly voice, "but you'll need to give us some time first. After all, we're still to deal with that other fellow you might have seen on your way in here, Cluny, did one of you say? His future will be brief, but great. The greatest honour lies before him, as it does for all of you. So, sit! You've seats. Rest those weary bones. Not everyone comes out breathing on the other side after taking on The Roof, and yet here all four of you remain on the *right* side of the Pits."

"Come a little closer, didn't quite catch all that," Marigold said, stumbling uneasily to the cell bars, dragging Haggar along with him.

"I think not. The chains stay on for now, the cells remain locked. Not all cells have seats, so enjoy what you have, it is more than adequate for the time being; you *did* attack us, after all."

The *seats* were little more than mounds of dirt dotted around. "Again, fuck you," Marigold growled, clenching the thick, metal bars.

"Ah, I try to offer kindness, but you throw it back in my face with coarse language," Lennan mumbled quickly, staring at Marigold along the end of his nose. "Now, to business. There are four of you behind these bars. Where is the fifth?"

"Dead," Magnus said.

"Hmm, yes. If I were incarcerated, I too would also claim that the one capable of breaking me out were dead or gone." Lennan smiled kindly. "Where is he?"

"He's dead, Lennan. One of your fucking creatures took him down." Marigold twisted at the rusting bars of the cell. With enough time he might well break one of these with his hands, but for now? He considered the distance between the cell limits and Lennan. Not even Marigold's arm was that long.

"My creatures? Hmm, we don't have any *creatures*. Perhaps you mean one of the parasites that plagues our Lord with itches and sores? Black? Somewhat spherical? Nasty bite?"

"Aye."

"Indeed, a parasite of our Lord. You see, this is why we tend to wear armour, though I've never personally felt I was in any danger from them and I've been down among them for many years now. A lesson learned for you, though, I suppose. Well, that settles that at any rate, I offer you my condolences." Lennan muttered something unintelligible into the ear of the cultist stood by him.

The caped fellow nodded in the affirmative and scurried off down the corridor.

"My friends," Lennan continued, "you really needn't worry about your captivity, we shan't hold you long." He turned to address another of the cultists in a low voice. "Run along and let the Captain know of the situation, and let's have another sweep along the routes for this dead fellow regardless."

The instructed man nodded at Lennan.

"Well? Be off with you, or must I go and inform him myself?" Lennan shrieked.

The fellow reddened and scuttled away, barging through the remaining entourage as he disappeared into the darkness.

"Imbecile," Lennan sighed. "You'd think taking orders would be the easy job, wouldn't you? Now, my friends, I'll leave you alone for a while. We'll bring you rations if the wait starts to draws out, but I shouldn't think you'll have the time to get *too* comfortable. Farewell for now!"

Lennan and the remainder of his men began to file out of the low-ceilinged cavern, melting into the gloom at the edge of the glow from the torch. The tramping of feet on sand faded soon after.

"What an absolute stoneless, cock welt of a fucking prick," Marigold stated.

"Aye," Magnus agreed.

"They're going to kill us, so they are, they are," Ramage whined, slumping down onto an uncomfortable looking rock. "That's it, we're done for. Dead!"

"You know what, Ramage?" Marigold began, staring out of the cell and grinding his palms into the bars tightly enough that the jagged rust began to eat into them, "I really thought you were something more than this. *You* approached *us* in the inn, if you remember, holding yourself high like you knew what the fuck you were doing, like a man that knows what he wants, a man not afraid to get his hands bloodied, or fight his enemies, or die trying. You've done the sum total of fuck all beyond whinge and whimper at just about damn well everything we've seen and pissing done since we began climbing this Pit-forsaken mountain! I'd have fucking left you there if I'd known!"

"I didn't think that-"

"Want me to snap his neck, Chief?" Magnus offered. "It'll be quick, quicker than what the rest of us'll get I'll bet."

"No, no, Magnus, we're more than outnumbered as it is. We need him yet, even if it's just as a meat shield. Bloody useless as anything else."

"I am," Ramage cried.

"What?" Marigold muttered, turning his swollen eye to the crestfallen woodcutter.

"Useless. I'm a coward, so I am," Ramage sobbed into his hands. "You know why me Ma is dead? She stepped in to save me when that bony bastard, Cecil, was about to cut me throat. All because I refused to go with them. Just rammed his hilt right into the side of her head, so he did. Dropped dead there on the leaves, no words, no cries. Dead. 'Live with that on your conscience,' Cecil told me, and then they left. You know why me entire family is gone to the cult? Because I stood there, piss dribblin' down me legs when they came for more of us last year. Had us all lined up. Gave us the chance to step forward, make it easier on everyone. Cecil and Russel were there, both of the bastards. Walked up and down the line, lifting chins, looking into eyes. Russel stopped by me, 'Come on, then,' he said. But I didn't, I fell to my knees, crying. Sara, me wife, me beautiful wife, she knelt by me but Russel dragged her up, put her with the others they were taking. Ike, he's m'wee son, ran to her and they took him too. Five, that's all he was. Taken for blessed Fyr knows what. I'm a coward, a fucking coward, alright? Didn't want to go because I didn't want to leave me family, so I didn't, and look what it got me? No family left at all! I should have been killed three times over already, so I should, and here I am, alone. Thought with you I'd be able to make something more of meself. I can't. It can't be done. I'll die a useless death."

Marigold shifted from foot to foot. He looked at Magnus, who was focusing hard on his hands. "Huh, fucking tooth in my knuckles," the bald hulk said. Marigold tried Haggar. The mute shot a quick, confused glance at his friend before studying the sand and stones of the floor.

Well... this was fucking awkward.

Marigold reluctantly turned to Ramage. Any hint of suspicion that the man might have had some involvement with the cult was dashed. The fellow was just a broken man, plain and simple, and while his face was still in his hands, he *was* looking at the group through the cracks between his fingers. What did the bloody man want? A hug and a kiss better? He was chained up in a cell with three bloody barbarians! Marigold wasn't the man to put a comforting arm around anyone, but he wasn't an arsehole. Ramage hadn't had a good time. "By fucking Greldin," the Chief finally groaned. He dragged his bound hands down his face. "Ramage, just... look, take a moment. Get yourself together. We didn't know the full story-"

"Nobody bloody asked!"

"No. We didn't, didn't really think we had to! So we're caged, yes, but it's not the first time for us and it won't be the last, for any of us." Was that good enough for a pep talk? Talking of a supposed future? Fuck, was he going to have to screen anyone he brought along with him in future? Test them for chances of mental breakdowns? "Cages don't hold barbarians for long, you'll see."

"Chief," Magnus whispered in Marigold's ear, "maybe I should... you know?" Magnus moved his hands in a twisting motion.

"No!" he hissed.

"So, just how *are* you planning on getting out," a weary, feminine voice asked from behind the group.

Marigold turned to face the cell next to theirs. "And just who in the flaming Pits are you?"

"Did you not hear Lennan when he mentioned me by name? Said I could tell you there were worse places to be kept? I'm Nina, long-term captive of the Crystal Order at your service. And he wasn't wrong, these are the finest lodgings I've had here."

"I didn't hear that, no," Marigold huffed. "I was thinking more about crushing his ancient fucking skull."

"Understandable," agreed Nina. The woman emerged from a dark corner of her cell and pulled back a rotten cut of brown fabric from her head. She was a pretty, if rather emaciated woman. Short and with delicate features, rings encircled her dark eyes, and unkempt black hair grew at uneven lengths around her dirty face. Had to be approaching thirty or so winters, or else her captivity had aged her.

Chains rattled as Haggar moved across the cell to get a better look. The man was a bloody monster.

"How long've you been down here, then?" Magnus asked, with all the nonchalance of discussing nothing more than the last meal they ate.

"You know, I really haven't a clue without the sun and moons to tell me. No diary, you see." She flourished open palms to the men. "Winter was giving way to the new buds of spring when I arrived at Elsdale."

"It's deep winter now," Magnus confirmed.

"Is that it?" she sighed, sitting on a rock by the metal bars that divided the group. Her brown sack coverings folded in as she bent down, confirming a severely malnourished frame. "Unless several have passed, of course… Honestly, it feels like I've spent longer in here than I ever did outside."

Magnus turned away and gripped the bars at the front of the cell. He was joined by Haggar, and the pair of them yanked and tugged amidst grunts and groans. Decent bars, all told.

"They're rather solid," Nina said, looking at her feet. "They won't budge. But don't worry, I've no doubt that you'll all get out. The last lot got out, too."

"How?" Marigold asked, interest piqued.

"The same way everyone gets out. Taken by the Order to meet their end with the Order's lord."

"And just who in the blue fuck is this shitting lord everyone keeps bringing up?" Marigold growled.

"Well, it's not Lennan," Nina chuckled. "Nor is it *Captain Cecil*," she waggled her fingers in mock awe, "or his son Russel, or any of that caped rabble that call themselves an Order."

"By Greldin, I'll tear them all limb from fucking limb before they drag me to meet this other bastard. And where in the Pits are all the others from Elsdale? They've had hundreds down here if what I've heard is right."

"I don't suppose you've tried inside the worm?"

"What bloody worm? What are you blathering about?"

"You're making a game of me, right?" Nina sneered as a grin lit up her face. Whatever she was finding so funny, it looked to be the first mirth she'd experienced in ages and she wasn't missing the chance to enjoy it.

"What pissing worm?" Marigold repeated, impatience getting the better of him as it so often did.

"The one that's all worm from mountain floor to mountain bloody ceiling! The *lord* this Order worships, though I question its ability to think of anything beyond base instinct," Nina shot back.

"What?" Marigold beat the bars separating them. "What are you damn well talking about, woman?"

The only sounds were crumbling rust fragments tapping the rock.

"Answer him!" Magnus prompted.

"Aye, just make it worse, can it even get any worse?" Ramage wept into his palms.

Eventually, Nina sighed. "The glowy blue thing that takes up most of this Gods-forsaken mountain? Don't tell me you made it down here without seeing it?"

"No we saw… Th-that's a…" Marigold didn't stammer or stutter, Marigold always knew exactly what he wanted to say. Only this was unexpected. A worm? He wasn't entirely sure that this little upstart wasn't making a game of *him*. A worm? A small, white, wriggling grub?

"W-What did you think it was?" That was genuine disbelief in her tone.

"Chief thought it was a tower, girl. A tower with a wizard at the top," Magnus grinned from the bars he still held. "Wizard that couldn't decide whether his staff or his cock was bigger, ain't that right, Chief? To be fair, we all thought that. You don't really expect *worms*, do you?"

Nina's stony gaze split into a grin. Less sarcasm, more simple amusement. Her hands leapt to conceal the snicker breaking though her lips and failed. She slid back against the rock of her cell and onto the sand. "A wizard? Ha! An actual wizard?" The giggling fit began in earnest, grew and grew until it was doused with pants and snorts. The barbarians grimaced as they glanced at one another. She breathed deeply and made an 'O' with her lips. "And just what wizard, Barbarian, would build a bright blue 'tower' like that, give it a pulse, then hide it away inside a bloody mountain?"

"Well, we all wondered the same thing," Marigold said, dejectedly, tugging at the barely braided tip of his beard with embarrassment. Flakes of dried blood dusted out of it.

"Well, it's not a wizard, it's a worm. A big worm. A rakeworm, if you must know. And a rakeworm that is probably quite close to hatching given the strength of the rumblings it's been making of late; nearly shook the roof of this tomb down upon me."

"Tomb? Don't they want you? Thought this worm was the tomb."

"I'm a special case, I'm afraid. I've seen men, women, children, all come and go. Lost count. They'll leave me here. They feed me now and then so I can stay around to witness it all – well, the excuse they call food – but once their Lord has hatched and burrowed away into the earth, they'll move on to the next one and leave me here to starve."

Marigold was confused. "Why in the Pits would they do that? You not good enough to be worm food?"

"No."

"Explain," Marigold demanded. "How do we get to be like you?" There was more chance of eventually chipping out of this cell than there was a colossal mouth.

Nina drew breath and let it out in a long sigh. "None of you are feminine enough to convince them you're *exactly* like me. This rabble, this Crystal Order, they worship rakeworms, see? Huge beasts, biggest creatures in Traverne. Big enough to seem *godly*."

"They like big," Ramage muttered.

"So you've met The Roof? You're lucky to be alive. But yes, huge, g*ods*. The cult've made it their business to seek out the cocoons of the young worms around Traverne to ensure that each one hatches successfully. That, in and of itself, would be no great problem. But the Crystal Order favours a more hands-on approach than simply waiting for the cursed things to slip out of their shells. To them, these brainless worms are nature's finest.

They are, after all, the biggest creatures that inhabit our world, and from what we can gather, they're among the original inhabitants too, not brought in from any Pit realm or portal. The reason Traverne is here, is for *them*. So the Order believe, anyway. It's all nonsense. The Order consider it a great honour to guarantee that all rakeworms are born fighting fit, and to that end, they feed them up. They believe there is some greater plan in place for those that do so. Fodder is what your people of Elsdale have become."

Ramage convulsed in his sobbing.

"I'm sorry, but it's the truth," she dismissed. "Now, the problem with feeding these rakeworms up is that they grow much faster and are born bigger than they ever have a right to be. Much bigger. A rakeworm usually remains within its cocoon for up to a century, but with the Crystal Order poking about they are birthing in half that time and at almost twice the size they should be thanks to a diet of flesh rather than dirt. More worms are out there, more cocoons are made, the Order spreads. More people are made food, and we're starting to see a rakeworm epidemic in the seas of home."

"I've never even heard of these worms. Mag, Hag: you?"

Heads shook.

"There are a number of reasons for that, my muscular friend."

"Marigold."

"Hmph. Very well, *Marigold*." She tasted the word for a moment. Recognition or mockery? Neither was entirely unexpected, really. "The worms remain out of sight for almost their entire lives, fixed in their cocoons in caves or hollow mountains until they hatch. When the Order root them out they sacrifice just about everyone in the vicinity of a cocoon, and thanks to their skill," she spat, "and the worms' propensity to lay eggs in the more difficult regions of the world, word doesn't spread by sight nor sound. A general lone investigator is likely to be killed by the caped bastards or one of those vile parasites the worms carry. Perhaps they end up simply fed to the worm. What's more, once hatched, the worms never break the surface of land. Rather, they travel out to the Birth Sea, churning the silty sea bed in their inexorable hunt to sate the hunger this cult has given them.

"I travelled here from one of the many islands that encircle the Birth Sea: Niihua, if you've heard of it. Our livelihoods are based on our ability to fish. The Empty Ocean to the south is no place for our skiffs to travel, no, we haul what we need in from the relative safety of inner Birth Sea. In the last few centuries, our families have suffered a vast reduction in the number of fish caught: and on the other side, a great increase in rakeworms. The worms are eating the fish faster than we can catch them. With more rakeworms foraging the ocean floor, there are times when territory comes into play. Fighting rakeworms are nothing to be trifled with, believe me. People are killed in great waves, skiffs smashed and dragged below the surface in vortexes created by the swirling beasts. Tsunamis tear our villages from the coasts. Our people live on the water, but even we lack the strength to swim out of something like that.

"The families of the Birth Sea came together several generations ago in order to get to the bottom of this increase in worms. It didn't take us long to discover the Crystal Order, for our initial investigations had us seek out the birthing chambers of the creatures. We had thought that perhaps the worms had begun to make two cocoons, but instead we found a youngling being force-fed terrified humans. The plan of action became quite simple after that; the Brethren remain along the archipelago and continue to fish and hunt rakeworms, while the Sistren make it their business to travel the world in search of rakeworm cocoons and rumours of the Order."

"Some story," Marigold said, scratching his head. "So, what is it you do when you find a worm? Just sit and watch it? I don't doubt you've some fight in you, but a slight little thing like you doesn't seem like the type to bring down something the size of this shitting rakeworm, or deal with the cult feeding it. Why don't you bring an army, or, if you haven't got one, tell an army?"

"We can't take down the Order, we know that. Their numbers are too great and always seem to be growing – there really are some impressionable fools out there – but, one person alone can sneak in where an army would be spotted immediately. It is dangerous work, but the role of the Sistren is to infiltrate and dispatch. Besides, the Crystal Order began in the Birth Sea, with a survivor of a worm attack who saw more in his survival than dumb luck – the man was swallowed out at sea and somehow lived long enough to end up at a cocoon laying – and before it all gets out of hand and the world finds out, we'd rather clean up the mess our own idiots made in relative secrecy."

"*By Greldin,* woman," Marigold growled, not up for the tale's meanderings at all, "I think it's more than out of hand at this point. What I want to know is if we can't avoid the big bastard worm, how do we take it down?"

"With this." Nina produced a small pouch from within the folds of the fabric that covered her. "It doesn't take much, and it is benign to most creatures of Traverne, but to a rakeworm, it is a swift end…" she tailed off, staring intently at the small bundle.

"Well, what happened then?"

"I…" Nina sighed again, cupped a hand over her mouth. "I lost conviction. I was there, stood below the maw of the creature, looking up into it, ready for it to take me inside."

"Take you… what? You were going to let it eat you?"

"Well, as you said, I am very small, and it is very large. The worm won't just eat this pouch, we need to get it deep inside them. The Sistren understand their lot in life. There is no shortage of women on the Birth Sea. By sacrificing ourselves, we are reducing the number of rakeworms at little cost to our population. A dead rakeworm means one less beast in the sea, means that the Crystal Order move on and leave the place they infest alone. Many stand to benefit from the sacrifice of one."

"You do realise you sound like part of a cult, now?"

"I do?" Nina took a step back, glanced at her body.

"You do. Anyway, why the change of heart? Why did you fail?"

"We are far from the Birth Sea, Marigold. I have travelled alone for a long time. On my travels I spent a great deal of time in Rumiruna, and while I was there, I met someone. We spent time together, and I almost lost my way as a woman of the Sistren. A different life began to blossom. It was difficult – very difficult – but one morning, I left. No note, no goodbyes. My time in Rumiruna had revealed clues that the cult were also down here, so that's where I went, to hunt down what I believed would have been the seventeenth rakeworm killed by the Sistren – had I been successful. When I found myself below the worm, I couldn't help but think about the person I left. There was the beast, mouth open, drool splashing me as its awful tentacles thrashed around. And yet, I hesitated." Nina began to pace her cell, fingers began to scratch at an arm. "I didn't step below the maw. Lennan and his men appeared. That brutish Roof character snatched me up and carried me away. They stripped me down, threw me in here and gave me this delightful sack cloak."

"Well how've you still got that poison then?" Magnus asked, pursing his lips and furrowing his brow.

"Sorry, what was your name?"

"Magnus, Mag, *The Muscles*, don't care." Magnus smirked.

"Very kind of you to offer choices. Well, *Magnus*, a woman is blessed with more hiding places than a man, and as dangerous as the Crystal Order can be, they are not *that* type of people. Or at the very least they're just plain ignorant."

Marigold felt his chains tense as a low sniggering bubbled from behind. Haggar was there, grinning like an idiot, looking Nina up and down. The bastard even winked. Pity for Haggar, laughing was still too much for the tongueless welt to deal with. A fresh wave of blood dribbled over his lips and down his chin.

"Vile," Nina uttered, shuddering somewhat.

"That's enough, Haggar, keep your eyes, your mouth, and your fucking tongue blood to yourself. Look, Nina, from what you say, we're in a bit of trouble now, but I'm still fairly sure that we'll get out of this one way or another. Hand over that poison and if it all does go to shit – somewhat literally, it seems – we can at least complete your mission for you."

"I'll do it, so I will," croaked Ramage from his rocky seat.

"You'll what?" Marigold asked with genuine surprise.

"I'll do it," he confirmed. "You heard what I said, last of me family, nothing to look forward to other'n me own inadequacies. At least let me go out doing some good. Besides, I don't have to aim when I'm the missile, eh?"

Marigold had to agree with that. "Fine by me. Better that than Nina dying down here for nothing, I say. Nina, you'll do this?"

"Well, I'm not going to get another chance. I've failed already. Sure," she shrugged. "Why not." Nina passed the small pouch to Marigold. The skin bag, tied shut with a black string, looked small in his palm. It was very round though, couldn't have been comfortable when stowed. "Nina," he asked, furrowing his brow. "Why didn't you force this fucking pouch into the hand of the first person that took up residence in the cell next to you?"

"You know what is going to happen to you, no? Have I not explained it well enough?"

Marigold glared at her.

"You barbarians, you're the first to sit in these cells and not spend your entire time here blubbering into your hands for some non-existent deity to save them. Well, three of you are. I tried to pass this on to the first few *companions* I was given, but I gave up shortly after. Barely any of them ever spoke to me, and those that did refused to accept what was coming."

"Fair enough." He passed the poison to Ramage, clinking and rattling chains. The woodcutter dropped it into one of the pockets of his overcoat and stared curiously at the little bulge in the dim light. The herald of the end. Given Ramage's earlier outburst, he was taking it all quite well. Perhaps there was some hope for the fucker yet, no matter how short-lived his time might be.

"Right," Marigold said, moving to the middle of the cell. "So, we have a plan. It's not the best, as plans go, but maybe it won't mean the end for all of us."

"I suppose we just wait, then, Chief?"

"I suppose we do."

Outside, in the main cavern, a deafening groan of ecstasy rose. The walls rumbled.

"That'll be the latest one from Elsdale," Nina said.

Ramage whimpered.

It could have been minutes, hours, or days. Down here in the dark cells, the only way in which Marigold was even aware that time was passing was with the slowly dwindling light of the torch beyond the cells. Pretty soon, that thing was going run out of fuel and then it would be darkness for the lot of them. No Cerulean Hair grew down here.

Haggar was sat on the sand, pawing at his mouth, and groaning each time his fingers touched something tender.

"Stop playing with it," chided Marigold, though only half-heartedly; if it helped his friend pass the time, what did it matter? That tongue wasn't growing back, no matter what he did, and pretty soon they'd all be rotting in the stomach of a Pit-spawned fucking worm anyway. Worm food. Fucking worm food. Marigold had often thought about the way in which he might leave this world for Greldin's Halls, but not one of his wildest imaginings had involved him and his friends fizzing away in the belly of some over-sized pissing maggot. There probably wouldn't even be any bones, and you couldn't really bury soup, or determine what parts would go in which hole. Who of the clan knew that any of them were even down here anyway? This was a proper fuck up. The kind of fuck up you didn't get to learn from. The kind of fuck up he had told Pettar to avoid. Perhaps one of his clan would eventually end up in Elsdale and find out just where Marigold had taken Magnus and Haggar and Pettar. Poor Pettar, killed for nothing. Perhaps someday the clan would avenge him. Marigold would most certainly be remembered by his clan. The Idiot Chief. What not to do if you wanted to run the gang for more than a few weeks. At least the clan now had a chance to go on with someone that had a little more sense to be in charge with.

The torch hissed out.

"Well, that's just fucking great," Magnus said.

"If you're down here any length of time you'll get used it, Magnus," Nina said from the corner of her cell. "A torch is a rarity, you should thank yourselves lucky you even got one."

"Very lucky," Magnus grumbled.

A high-pitched clicking began to sound just outside the cells.

"The fuck is that?" Marigold spat, pacing to the front of the cell and dragging Haggar up with him. His eyes strained, he couldn't see a damn thing in this darkness.

"One of the rakeworm's ticks. The parasites that Lennan mentioned. Don't worry, they can't squeeze into the cells. If anything, they just add some variation to the monotony down here," Nina finished dryly.

"Well that variation is what killed our lad, Pettar. If it comes anywhere near these bars I'll rip its bloody jaws off."

"Very manly."

Marigold snorted with disgust, though he stepped back from the bars nonetheless.

Footsteps sounded from within the inky depths. A deep orange glow became yellow, became the flickering warmth of a new torch. The clicking sounds scattered as the forms of many robed cultists filed into the open space before the cells. Lennan pushed his way to the front of the crowd.

"Did you all have a nice rest?" he asked, with what sounded like genuine curiosity. "Our checks have been thorough and you really are all quite alone here, aren't you?" Lennan leaned in. "Lucky for us," he whispered. "Our Lord, however, is restless, He hungers for His final meal. You may yet live to feel yourselves sink deep within the earth as He delves deep from His cocoon. You should be proud."

"Your worm is a she, fool," barked Nina.

"Oh, I rather doubt that. Such majesty, such size, is befitting only of the male of the species."

"Whatever you say, Priest."

"And I do say," replied Lennan. "Now then, you," he jabbed the arm of the cultist next to him, "unlock those cells and have them out. I trust that none of you will try anything stupid? The Roof is awaiting us all at the mouth of this cave, and he won't take kindly to any bloodshed that he hasn't caused himself."

"We won't try anything, Lennan, you can be assured of that," Marigold said calmly. "I think we're all quite eager to meet this wriggling lord of yours. After all, it's not every day you find yourself face to maw with a pissing rakeworm, is it?"

"Bravo! Have you had fun educating the simple folk, Nina?" Lennan asked, clapping his hands together. He stood to one side as the three barbarians and the woodcutter were led out of the cell. "Farewell, Nina," he called back as the group shuffled back into the narrow cave. "This might be the last of our meetings."

"I should be so lucky," she called back.

Chapter Seven

THE STINKING BREATH OF DIVINITY

Sure enough, The Roof was waiting gormlessly for the procession in the relative open of the cavern. The hulking mass of flesh and muscle swayed gently from foot to foot, gazing stupidly through lank strings of black hair at the blue glow of the tower – the *cocoon* – as though it was somehow mesmerising him with its slow pulse and shimmering. Maybe it was. Maybe everyone down here was under its thrall.

"Least we'll find our way into the fucker this time, eh?" Magnus laughed from behind Marigold.

"We will indeed. Always good to look on the bright side," Marigold deadpanned. The bright blue and glowy side, in this case.

The chains linking the men by the wrists trembled as the group were led out of the cell tunnel and back into the subterranean home of the rakeworm. Lennan led the way, while The Roof was given control of the chains. No point trying to yank their way out this one; The Roof would have all four of them swinging in a whirl over his head. Strong bastard, that Roof. Unfairly strong. Marigold was the first in line, flanked by four blue-caped cunts on either side. He would probably be the first to go, and that only seemed right given that he got everyone into this mess. His heavy chains dangled between his legs, trailing underneath him and bashing him in the stones every now and then. Wasn't death enough? Did they have to add that too? Haggar took up the chains behind. Beyond, Magnus looked around the place as calmly as The Roof for some unknown reason. Ramage brought up the rear and he seemed to be the source of the shaking in the chains. That was fair enough; it had to have taken some guts for the local man to agree to what was essentially suicide, even if they were all but guaranteed death regardless now. Those guts had fled him very quickly, all told. Marigold watched the woodcutter until his neck ached too much. What did such intense fear feel like? Marigold was angry, but he didn't feel fear. If the end came, it fucking came. It wasn't that he didn't care – he was actually very pissed off at the way this had all turned out – but he'd had a good and full life, if he ignored the years wasted at the beginning. He had killed more wizards, witches, sorcerers, and other assorted ringpieces than he could count on the fingers and toes of himself and any of the men chained to him combined. He had slain creatures the world didn't know existed – fitting that he was about to be eaten by one – and somehow had also managed to become the chief of a clan he had only been running with for half of his life, although that last part hadn't really worked out. The biggest shame was that he wouldn't get where he wanted to be with Elvi. Still, he'd meet her again in Greldin's Halls, and she would remember him.

But…

He was still breathing. Still walking. He couldn't start worrying about what he was going to miss until he was sat firmly on a stone seat by Greldin him-fucking-self. Marigold never assumed that a suspected end would ever actually *be* the end. That was the key to surviving, and it hadn't failed him yet.

Bored of staring at The Roof's muscular arse, the chief looked back at his men again, pulling the skin around his bruised eye socket taut. Shit, it hurt. He'd had some black eyes before, but he suspected some serious fractures dwelt beneath this one. Caped men and women began to emerge from the hundreds of dark holes in the rock, joining the procession. A buzz hung in the tepid air, a murmuring of a community. Who knew how big the network of tunnels down here might really be? Or how many more cultists they might hide. There were capes ahead, to his side, and behind him. Capes fucking everywhere, but not even half the amount now that there had been when The Roof had put them down. Bloody embarrassing. If only that particular memory had been knocked out of him along with all the others he no longer knew he once knew.

If you can't forget, you focus on something else. It was the cocoon's turn to take the eye of Marigold. Now that he really looked at it, it was fucking obvious it was the stinking shell of some damn creature. He could even see the pale bastard writhing within the opaque barrier. It pulsed with a slow heartbeat, it glowed. Of course the bloody thing was alive. Marigold had just *wanted* it to be a tower. He had *wanted* there to be a wizard sat at the top. It was nice and easy to blame anything on magic. Magic was something that he could deal with. A rumbling mountain? Magic! A dead friend? Magic! A giant fucking man that could knock out three barbarians and a woodcutter without even breaking sweat? Well, that was definitely magic, and if those swirly ethereal strings hadn't been involved somewhere in The Roof's conception, then the stones that spawned him were among the most potent to have ever existed.

Probably even rivalled his own.

The best part about blaming something on magic was that there was nearly always some fool with the ability to cast the stuff somewhere nearby. There probably *was* at least one in this cave, even if it wasn't the antagonist of the moment. Magic was rife in

Traverne: it was everywhere Marigold went, one way or another. Fuck's sake, there were even folk out there with an ability and they didn't even know they had it. Powder kegs waiting to go off. Slaying a mage was a fine way to get to the 'bottom' of a problem, whether or not they were actually responsible. Their severed heads were almost always enough to convince someone that whatever it was that *had* troubled them, it would trouble them no more. Marigold ran through the faces of each and every one that had fallen to his hands, feet, teeth, and sword. If this rakeworm really was to be the end then he might as well remember the good times that brought him here.

Marigold looked back at the wizard-less cocoon and sighed. Shame how things turned out. His gaze drifted from the pounding blue shaft to the pale blue headdress that wobbled atop Lennan ahead. The man called himself a 'High Priest', whatever that entailed. Just a cult title, no real indication of any magical abilities but it could be worked with. Marigold had met priests that could cast a spell before, but Marigold doubted that this frail old git really possessed any such sort of knowledge or they'd have found out about it first-hand. Whatever, the bastard was going to have to do for now, and there could be no harm done in simply removing him as a precaution.

"Get the fuck off me, shithead."

Marigold jerked his head back to see Magnus kicking a cultist to the ground. "Hey! Not now!" he warned.

"Fine," he spat. "Keep your fucking hands to yourself," Magnus sent a cascade of sandy dirt over the fellow struggling to get back up. "You'll be choking on them if they touch me again."

An irritated grunt came from the very front of the procession.

"Easy now," Lennan soothed The Roof. His wizened hand found the chain bearer's thigh and stroked it gently. The Roof audibly relaxed and resumed his heavy stomping. The jerk on the chains almost dragged Marigold off his feet. The slow thud of metal boots on sand beat in time with the rakeworm's heart. "There's a good boy."

By Greldin, it was a *dreary* trudge. Absolute madness that walking to one's death could be tedious. Past a patch of red sand they trudged, the spot where barbarian blood had been spilled in the earlier scuffle. Past the streams and the pools, around the back of the cocoon. Back to where Marigold and his men had first searched for a way into what they had believed to be a tower. If there really was some fucking door back here, Marigold was going to bloody scream.

In the space behind the worm tower, in the darker recesses of this vast, hollow mountain, a collection of dark and jagged rocks formed a semicircle a short distance from the cocoon. Lennan, the old bastard, was almost skipping. He had The Roof pass the chains to one of his cultists and bounded ahead of the group. The old priest cast two stones together with a sharp crack, the sparks lit two clumps of dried Cerulean Hair that were placed on the tops of each side of the stone semi-circle. The new glow revealed another cave below that had been hidden within the darkness of shadow. A descent beneath the sand. It wasn't a small aperture either. Marigold tutted to himself as he and the others were ushered towards it. They had been looking for a way into the bright blue shaft, sure, but how one of them hadn't noticed this bloody arrangement was beyond him.

"In you go, in you go," Lennan laughed excitedly, hopping from foot to foot like some impatient child awaiting a sweet treat. The fool really was quite unhinged. "Can't keep our Lord waiting, can we? None of us wish to be on His bad side, a-a-ahaha. Just look at the size of Him!" His eyes followed the edge of the cocoon. "Vast! Magnificent! Hungry! And you are all so small, but... But, you'll do. You'll all do."

The caped bastards ahead jerked the group along. Marigold considered kicking the priest in the stones as he passed him, but decided it would have been too much of a chore to locate any such organ beneath that billowing white cloak.

Wide and flat cuts of black stone formed steps down into this new space. Immediately, a hot and rancid stench invaded Marigold's nose. A taste of rotting meat basted his tongue, the heat stung his eyes. No wonder the inside of Spitertind was so warm; this bastard worm was a fucking furnace. The tunnel was carved high. High enough that it had obviously been made with The Roof in mind. Marigold could understand why, to an extent. Down here was a butcher's yard. A slaughterhouse. The method of execution might differ from the ways he knew, but this was a place of death, make no mistake. These steps were the last steps that each of the missing men, women, and children had taken before being consumed by an oversized maggot. A shit way to go for anybody. Fucking shit. How many of the condemned had tried to escape? How many lives had ended at the fists of that hulk? Marigold spat into the gloom.

The tunnel grew steadily darker. Marigold felt a shadow creeping along his back. The Roof had entered – remarkably delicately – and any notion of escaping the way they had entered was gone. The darkness made the blue glow ahead plain to see. The steps came to an end, and the doomed men were dragged along. Magnus grumbled, Ramage whimpered. Only Greldin knew what Haggar was thinking, and it hurt too much for Marigold to bother looking back to find out. Each step felt heavier than the last. The chances of getting out of this mess were looking slimmer by the second. Marigold's stomach churned. For once, he really was beginning to consider what death was going to be like. That wasn't good. It still wasn't time to give up.

"Come on, come on," Lennan shrieked, barging past the group and rushing on ahead.

Marigold watched the white streak break out into a wider section of the cave. The priest took careful steps to one side and stepped back, holding his headdress in place as he looked upwards in reverence. Naturally, Marigold's eyes followed suit.

There it was. There was the end. The first real look at what passed for divinity in this place.

The great and sickening maw of the rakeworm formed the ceiling of this humid cavern. A huge circle of flesh leering over the packed dirt below. It was high enough up that even The Roof would be able to walk below it if he wished. He probably didn't, but then that would require him thinking for himself. The glowing blue edges of the base of the cocoon provided the haunting bloom that lit up the feeding grounds. Pallid, white flesh poked out from behind it, a quivering horizontal curtain of worm lips, if worms actually had lips. Whatever they were, they blackened as they neared the centre. The opening. As the procession filed into the grotto that black flesh withdrew with a snap. Animal instinct. Food was here. The edges slackened as the… the lips, were drawn back to reveal the pink and moist inside of the rakeworm's mouth. Rows of miniscule, white teeth encircled the maw at the very edges, joined by flaps of twisting, pink organs that stretched out and flopped back as the worm rippled in anticipation. Looked like nothing more than a collection of soft cocks along the edges, and the middle looked closer to a ruined arse than a mouth. Could it get any worse than that? Great globs of clear juice slid out over the edges of the white flesh, hissing as it met with the stone and sand below.

Fuck.

Marigold had never considered that a worm could salivate, but there it was, drooling away. A bass noise rose and faded in fits and starts. Hot air rushed out from the mouth in waves, blowing tangled hair from Marigold's face and plastering it elsewhere with the moisture in the draught. The worm was panting, waiting, excited. It knew its next meal had arrived. The fucking thing's breath stunk like a rotting rukh, and was as hot as a desert wind to boot.

Marigold swallowed as he was lined up on the edge below the worm, near a wildly animated Lennan. They were just away from standing directly below the enormous mouth. Marigold looked along the chains to his friends. Haggar, Magnus, and Ramage's eyes were all affixed to the rippling flesh above. Ramage shook violently. Marigold was tensing muscles so that he didn't do the same.

Marigold searched the cavern from where he stood. Anything that could be useful now was vital. It was a long way to the other side, and the worm's circular gob covered almost the entirety of the empty space below it. Empty for a good bloody reason. The very far edges were surrounded by a moat of sorts that encircled the entire space. Armed cultists continued to file in, creating a human circle beneath the worm. The Roof plodded to a stop behind Lennan. Enemies to the sides, behind, and some supposed divine beast above. They were trapped, all of them. Lennan's men had had years of practice at this, and it didn't seem like they had let a meal escape yet.

"Welcome to the Table," Lennan said solemnly, and with a wide sweep of his arms.

An actual dining table for the worm, then. Well, at least The Roof didn't have a fucking brother.

The last of the caped cultists arrived. Silence, save for the inexorable panting of the great mouth above, filled this vision of hell and the end.

"Shall we begin?"

The cultists encircling the Table knelt in unison, a metallic clattering as armoured knees went to the dirt and stone. "*Begin*," they cried together.

"Join with us now," Lennan cried in reverential tones. "Take within you this feast of flesh."

"*Feast of flesh,*" the cultists chanted together.

"Your body shall be birthed afresh."

"*Birthed afresh.*"

"O, Great Rakeworm, burrow deep."

"*Burrow deep.*"

"Return to us an egg to keep."

"*An egg to keep.*"

"Feast now, Rakeworm! Feast! Feast!"

"*Feast! Feast! Feast!*"

Classic cult chanting, weird fuckers. The animal smelt food, it wasn't waiting for these halfwits to finish their worship.

The rakeworm's lips unfurled back over their edges. The monster barked a vile cough, showering all with hot, hissing saliva. The cavern shook, dust crumbled from the walls, the moat around the edges sloshed and rippled. Cultists and victims alike steadied themselves.

"So that's what a god looks like, eh?" Magnus called out over the din of excitement. "Reckon Greldin's as tall as that, Chief?"

"We're about to find out," Marigold muttered.

"A chief? As in a real, barbarian chief?" Lennan squealed, leaning around to get a better look at Marigold.

"Aye," Marigold said, curling his lips.

"Oh, oh, oh! We really *did* save the best meal for last. Do you hear that, friends? This man is a chief! A fine dessert indeed. I can feel it!"

"*We feel it!*" the cult chanted.

"This is the one! Our Lord will drop from His cocoon tonight!"

The roar of exultation was thunder, drowning out all but the deepest of rumbles from the rakeworm.

Ramage stepped forward slightly. The chains jangled as the woodcutter took an uneasy breath and looked Marigold directly in the eye. Marigold gently nodded back.

"Quickly now," Lennan ordered. "Watch the tendrils, men. Seems the local would like to go first, how very brave of him."

Marigold didn't like that tone.

Ramage's head darted left and right, eyes wide with terror. Clearly, he was still hoping for some kind of deliverance from his final moments. His mouth opened soundlessly as three of the cultists hastily undid the shackles from his wrists. The metal hit the ground, silent among the stamping of feet and the raging of the starving beast. The cult men dragged Ramage out of the line, ducking low as they hauled him over. Beneath the centre of the mouth they stood.

With a last dash of luck, perhaps Nina's poison would murder the monster before any more among them could be fed to it. Maybe it'd vomit up Ramage while he was still alive. The rasping from above seemed to reach a crescendo. No wonder the mountain fucking shook! Marigold saw a dark trail of liquid below Ramage.

Then the worst happened.

The fuckers tore the clothes from Ramage's body. They cut with knives. Yanked and pulled. Ramage was left standing naked but for his tattered underclothes. The pouch of poison, once in a pocket, was lost beneath the shreds of dyed animal skins piled at his feet

"Fuck me," Magnus groaned, "you wantin' to give him one last tug?"

Ramage looked back, teared eyes taking in all around him. No hope remained in them.

The pink nodes of flesh between gullet and teeth reddened and stiffened, engorged with blood.

Snap!

They lashed out. Tens of times the length they had been while just dangling there, the nodules were articulate limbs lunging for their prey. They wrapped around Ramage like constrictor snakes. In an instant the woodcutter was swept from the ground and up into the beast. His legs wriggled briefly from the centre of the throat, a black hole high up within the maw. Ramage disappeared amidst slurps and drips.

A hissing sigh came from the worm as the circle of cultists fell to their knees. Some bowed, some held their arms aloft. All looked ridiculous.

"There'll be less of that embarrassment for you, don't you worry – not that I believe any of you have anything to worry about in that regard, you're all fine figures of men," Lennan said from the side, pointing to the clothes. "The good thing about men like you, is that you wear very little. We can't be having our Lord consume something that might make him ill, can we?"

Marigold's arms jerked, just as he felt the massive hand of The Roof clamp his shoulder. His end was next up.

"We heard Nina, you know," Lennan continued. "Listen to her all the time. Can't have one of the Birth Sea Sistren here without keeping tabs on her and her attempts at seasoning the food, can we?" he chuckled.

"Come on then, you fuckers," Marigold said. "Might as well get this shit over and done with, eh?" He glanced at Haggar, and flicked his eyes to the side, gesturing as discreetly as he could to The Roof behind him.

Haggar gave the barest of nods.

"You ready for this?" Marigold called to Magnus.

"Yeah, Chief," he called back.

A plan formed between the three friends. The kind of wordless strategy that can only come about from sharing numerous terrible situations on a regular basis.

Without a moment's hesitation, Marigold jolted forwards, out from The Roof's grip, beneath the worm. The chains tightened between the barbarians. Immediately, cultists shot up from their knees, tottering on the edge of the circle, terrified of entering the death zone. The rakeworm bellowed. Marigold, Haggar, and Magnus stood back to back to back directly below the maw. A tight spot and no mistake. The lips drew back. One of the cult men stepped forwards and was instantly snatched by the tendrils. With a piercing scream the man was gone. Swords were unsheathed in a clamour of ringing metal. The Roof paced out from the circle, joining the barbarians below the worm.

"Son, get back here now!"

The Roof grunted.

"Right now!"

Pink flesh wrapped itself around The Roof's tree-trunk arms as he reached for Marigold and his men. The Roof jerked, tearing the organs from the worm's mouth as they remained coiled around his limbs, showering all four men in orange blood. The rakeworm roared and snapped its mouth shut.

"Come on," yelled Marigold, "let's have this fucking puppet!"

Marigold leapt at The Roof's considerable chest as Haggar and Magnus wrapped their chains around the legs. The bastards should have used shorter bonds. With his hands bound, it was all the Chief could do to simply pinch and hold onto The Roof's sweat-sheened pectorals. The goon's simple face glared at Marigold. Marigold responded by smashing his forehead into a nose the size of his own face. Cartilage and bone crunched and snapped beneath the blow, blood covered both men. In a moment of amazement, The Roof managed to affix both of his eyes onto Marigold for a single breath, sending a meaty hand to grip the Chief's back. The Roof wrenched Marigold from his chest. Haggar and Magnus, still joined to their leader, were dragged back, but Magnus gripped a thick thigh before he was flung up towards the worm. The overgrown man-child held the three muscle-bound barbarians with ease. Even in this state, Marigold had to admire his enemy's strength.

Cultists, wills reinforced by the iron display of strength from The Roof, began to filter into the dusty, slobbery circle below the worm. It sensed the nearby food and the mouth gaped once again. Men were plucked like ripe berries from a bush.

Snap!

Scream.
Snap!
Scream.

It was too much for the cultists to see their own demolished by the lord they so revered. This *god* didn't care about them. This *god* didn't know friend from food. The illusion was shattered. No longer did a deity hang above them. Now, a monster slathered and groaned for meat. Feet began to pound the ground as blue capes flicked the air and bodies made for the direction of the exit. The Roof, as unaware of who was on his side as the worm, began thrashing his comrades. Crushing spines with fists, snapping limbs, mulching skulls. Bodies were strewn everywhere, the cult cut down by their own. The rakeworm scooped up the living, the dead, it didn't care. Meat was meat, contrary to Lennan's teachings.

"Get back here!" Lennan shrieked. "Get back here at once, all hands to our Lord! Protect our Lord!" The priest stumbled onto his backside. He was old and frail, and pretty much useless in a fight, but it seemed that he wasn't planning on running away.

Magnus began pounding his knuckles into The Roof's stones. Magnus wasn't afraid to bring out the dirty moves in a desperate situation. Haggar bit into The Roof's arm, blood seeping from around his teeth. The monster-man's grip on Marigold weakened and the Chief was dropped. The chain caught on his massive forearms, dangling Marigold over the bloodied dirt. The rakeworm's roar threatened to tear his eardrums to shreds. Marigold kicked off The Roof's stomach. He scrambled back up the man, grabbing great clumps of flesh between his fingers. He'd done a lot of climbing in his life, but he'd never climbed a man. The basics were still the same, at least. As he clutched a fistful of The Roof's hair, Marigold cracked his forehead into his foe's right eye. The pain he caused himself almost cost him his grip. Marigold bit his lip, forced out the agony, and cast himself over the shoulder. The sheen of sweat between the men ensured he slithered around like a greased pig. A thick and salty residue filled his mouth as he used teeth to slow himself. Marigold managed to grab the excess chain whipped up from Magnus and dragged it taut around The Roof's neck. This was the opening they all needed.

The Roof gasped as the links tightened over his throat. Hands reached into the air, clutching at nothing. He began to stumble back.

The three barbarians clung onto The Roof as he staggered around the arena. The only cultists left around them now were maimed and dying below the worm.

Marigold positioned himself behind The Roof's head, guiding him towards the edge of the circle like he was breaking in a rukh. "Get the imbecile that way," he screamed. "Get him to the fucking water."

"Kill them!" squealed Lennan, shuffling on his arse, away from the brawl.

The Roof wailed. A sound very close to fear.

The moat shimmered in the blue light. Tantalisingly close. The worm's maw rapidly opened and shut. Tendrils snapped out like a cracking whip, clutching at nothing more than the stinking air. The beast groaned. The beast hungered. It wanted more.

The Roof hacked and coughed. "Da-da-ddy!" he cried with a bass bellow.

Haggar and Magnus dropped as closely to the floor as they were able. The chains connecting the three barbarians ate deeply into The Roof's flesh. Feet teetered over the very edge of the water. He bellowed a strangled cry, arms flailed to try and loose Marigold or Haggar or

Magnus. But the Chief and his men clung on, tightening the chains as much as they could. It was them, The Roof, or all fucking four of them. Just how big were this bastard's lungs? The goliath's eyes bulged, ready to leave their sockets.

From over his massive, sweaty shoulder, and greasy strands of black hair, Marigold caught Lennan creeping closer, staff raised. "Haggar, behind!"

Haggar, clinging to The Roof's knee, twisted his neck just in time to receive Lennan's white staff across his face.

The length of wood shattered on the mute's furrowed brow. Marigold watched as Lennan stumbled back in shock. Gems from the broken staff scattered across the cavern, skittering beneath the worm, plopping into the ring of water.

"Lost! Lost!" Lennan cried as he shuffled away on palms and feet. "All is lost, our Lord is-"

Marigold heard no more, for at that moment, his plan for The Roof reached its conclusion. Marigold crashed into the depths of the pool around The Table, still latched onto The Roof. For a moment, all was white. Bubbles rushed into his eyes and ears and nose. A huge fist slapped him across the face, amplified by the water. Marigold's grip on The Roof was lost. As he sunk deeper he saw Magnus and Haggar rapidly trying to untangle themselves from The Roof's legs. Muffled bellows and wobbling bubbles of escaped breath made plotting the next steps rather difficult. He had a decent reserve of air in his lungs, but that wasn't going to last forever. The plan hadn't gone as far as this.

His ribs felt tight.

As the water cleared of foamy bubbles, Marigold found himself face to face with The Roof again. One eye stared intently, the other closed beneath swollen flesh, but was probably looking somewhere else anyway. Marigold noted calmly the enormous hands attempting to crush him at the torso. He thrust his thumbs into The Roof's nose, but the water killed the force he needed. Marigold felt the bubbles leave his mouth and nose, felt them flutter over his eyes and dance through his swirling hair as they made their escape.

Fuck.

Then the pain moved, went below. His hands were being dragged down. Was The Roof packing a third arm and hand down there, among the stones? Dull thuds beat in the water. Marigold scanned through the bubbles down to see Magnus' hand rising up and disappearing into the darkness of The Roof's nether regions. Seemed Magnus really had taken this 'bigger than you' shit very personally. The pressure around Marigold's ribs disappeared amidst a muted bass wail of agony and sadness. Haggar jerked his Chief away.

Marigold broke the surface of the water with a ragged gasp. He dug his nails into the dirt and rock and hauled himself up with a roar. Foamy water slopped across The Table as Marigold's legs scrabbled for purchase. He turned back to the water and heaved with his bound hands. Haggar came up, a fresh wave of red streamed from his mouth and nose. He was still fucking beaming though. Madman. Together, Marigold and Haggar dragged Magnus up into... well, safety was hardly the word with that fucking worm writhing about above them. Magnus was also flashing his teeth.

"Fucking good, that, eh?" he said. "Massive stones. S'pose that's what you'd expect, though." He flexed the hand that had been used in the beating of them. "Almost too big for my hand," he mused.

Marigold tottered as he stood up, uneasily surveying the scene. Just the barbarians, the maggot, and the wreckage of the cult. The worm's mouth whipped open and shut, still desperate for more. Those hideous tentacles darted out, snatching impotently. Marigold strongly disliked tentacles. The colossal creature moaned. It knew they were there but it couldn't reach them, fixed as it was to its rigid cocoon. Marigold looked back down into the pool. The water was calming, now that they weren't thrashing about in it. The Roof just stood below the surface, staring up. Fucker's head was barely a hand's span from the surface, some of that hair – finally cleansed of its grease – floated at the surface in black swirls. But those metal boots and chains he wore seemed to be anchoring him down a treat. The huge bastard just stared at them all as they all looked back. There was a distinct look of fear in The Roof's eyes, but the imbecile didn't seem to have a clue as to how to escape. Perhaps this was to be the simpleton's first and last bath. A large bubble of air leaked from the giant's nose, and with that The Roof's eyes slowly closed for good.

"Looks like I'm back to counting just the one man bigger than me, Mag," Marigold said, patting his large friend on the shoulder with both of his chained hands.

"Too fucking right, Chief. Say, we getting rid of these chains or what?"

"Not yet." Marigold chewed the insides of shredded cheeks, the eyes of Haggar and Magnus on him as he stared at the vast mouth above them. "We're going to get that pissing woodcutter back."

Haggar and Magnus jangled their chains as they nodded grimly.

"That's why you're the Chief, Chief," Magnus said with approval.

"Grab something sharp. We're going inside it and I fucking intend on coming back out."

"It's a pity that shithead Lennan ran away, eh?" Magnus muttered as he bent down to retrieve a flimsy looking sword from the ground.

"Why?" Marigold asked.

"Well, he was the biggest prick of all, wasn't he?"

Marigold barked a laugh. He fucking was. Lennan was still on Marigold's 'to do' list. If nothing else, that was one reason for making sure he emerged from some part of this shitting rakeworm. He only hoped that it wasn't going to be its arse, or in the form of some shapeless slop.

Marigold crouched and led his two friends by the chains as they crept across The Table to the remains of Ramage's clothes. He collected a short knife along the way and slipped it into his belt. The pickings were slim, but the blade was sharp, and the inside of that worm's mouth looked soft. There was the pouch of poison, poking out from beneath a shred of leather. He remembered Nina saying that it was harmless to just about anything other than the worm. Nothing else for it, then. He popped the little bag in his mouth and clamped his teeth shut.

Marigold stood up below the centre of the maw, and nodded at Magnus and Haggar to do the same. "Cu on en, oo o-ergro schlug!" he bellowed around the pouch in his cheeks. Hot wind coursed around them as the mouth was wrenched open in response. Sticky saliva coated each of them, matting beards and hair to the skin, or creating a shining pate in the case of Magnus. This close up, the roar of the worm almost blew them down. Fuck's sake, it was loud. It wouldn't do for Haggar to lose both speech *and* hearing. By Greldin, if only this had been something as bloody simple as a wizard in a pissing tower.

This was a bad bloody idea.

"Let's give it the fucking shits!" Magnus yelled, as one of the oral tentacles snapped out from within, coiling around the big man's throat and ending his cry.

More feelers burst out, each one gripping limbs. They held tightly, tighter than the lock The Roof had had Marigold's ribs in.

The pink and fleshy mouth above quivered in delight.

Marigold, Haggar, and Magnus were wrenched from the floor in the blink of an eye. Snatched up. Taken deep within the stinking confines of the monstrous throat.

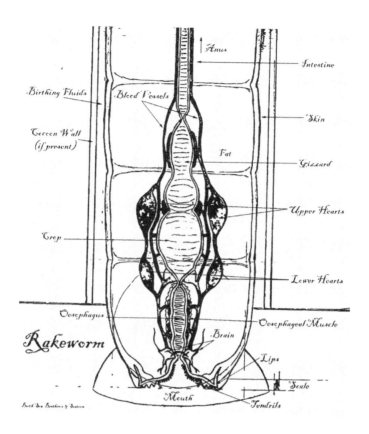

Rakeworm

Anus

Intestine

Birthing Fluids

Bleed Vessels

Screen Wall
(if present)

Skin

Fat

Gizzard

Upper Hearts

Crop

Lower Hearts

Oesophagus

Oesophageal Muscle

Brain

Lips

Scale

Mouth

Tendrils

Chapter Eight

A MEAL OF IT

Heat. Humid, sticky, suffocating heat.

Pinkish walls of muscular flesh gripped Marigold tightly, sending feverish shivers of disgust down his spine despite the uncomfortable warmth. The dull shaft was enormous yet claustrophobic and darkened rapidly as the... *lips* below closed themselves shut. All that remained was black, slime, and the sensation of being dragged upwards while being powerless to stop it. Breathing was hot and ineffectual and painful, and was certainly not helped by the pouch of poison he'd filled his mouth with.

Time was running out for all of them. By Greldin, it better not have run out for Ramage already. It couldn't have been more than a couple of minutes before the poor bastard was slurped up inside this fucking mutant. He couldn't be that much further up ahead.

But what to do? For once, Marigold didn't really have any previous experiences that he could draw upon. It was like his beginnings all over again. Up he slid, unable to fight back. His hands, arms, shoulders... they felt like they were close to being ripped off as they dragged Haggar and Magnus up from below. Up towards death. Up to the awaiting stomach, or whatever the fuck it was that a rakeworm held within it. Moans came from Magnus, even Haggar. Up they jerked again. They were like unusually small children gripped by an oddly larger than average adult. One that was a tad stronger than The Roof. None of them had expected this kind of power from the worm. Well, what in the Pits had they expected? Heartbeat pounded on heartbeat somewhere deeper within. A slow-ticking clock counting down to the inevitable.

In the history of Marigold's bad ideas – and there had been a fair few – this had to take the top spot as the very worst. And the most stupid. There they had been, worrying about being eaten by this fucker and then digested in what was likely to be one of the most agonising and awful ways to die, and now they had all voluntarily fed themselves to this colossal bloody slug, this giant fucking column of flesh and nodules and death. Saving the woodcutter... What had Marigold been thinking? But that look in Ramage's eyes before he was taken in. The poor bastard hadn't had a particularly enjoyable life by the sounds of things, and being melted in stomach acid would be a shit way for it all to end. The man needed to go out on a high, just not high up in a worm. By Greldin, Marigold was a barbarian, not a bastard! Of course, he was going to rescue the cunt. He had to do something right today.

The narrow throat convulsed and Marigold was dragged deeper into the beast. The words *'not over yet'* whirled around his mind, becoming fainter with each pass. The pouch of poison in his mouth was causing him to salivate profusely. He resisted the urge to swallow, and pushed the little bag to his front teeth with his tongue. He held it tight. He needed to know how his men were, but whether he ended up in that stomach or not, that poison was definitely going to be delivered.

"Agnush, Aggar?" he mumbled through the obstacle over his tongue. Couldn't open his mouth much, couldn't drop the poison now. Marigold glared down into the black abyss. Fuck, it was almost airless in this sack of flesh. Words were going to have to be limited to conserve what little air remained.

"Fine, Chief, you good?" came the muffled reply.

"Righ'. Uff. Don' cu' yeck, lesh ge' Rawage." Man alive, this was ridiculous.

"Umm, aye."

Marigold let the poison bag fall back between his cheeks. He felt the pressure in his arms lessen as the men below did their utmost to force themselves up through the endless tunnel that was the rakeworm's throat. Brave bastards. How high were they by now?

Another lurch simultaneously squashed and thrust them upwards. Marigold's head hit something hard. Metal. Armour. "Unng… ung'eed 'andsh," he called back. Marigold pushed his legs out into the sides of the squishy passage as impromptu brakes. Wet and slimy. The skin of his bare chest began to prickle. Digestive juices were flowing down over them. Here was the fucking warm up. The basting. *Fuck, fucking, fucking, fuck!* It itched something fierce. Another obstacle trying to reduce the window of opportunity that was rapidly closing. As Marigold put his all into holding himself in place within the slimy, shuddering throat, Haggar came up between his knees. An absurd shitting situation. This was another one of those occasions where he was going to have to agree with the men that they would tell the tale differently if they ever got out of it. Hands semi-free, Marigold explored the object above him.

Boots.

"On' ov vemsh above. Ungno' Rawage." Marigold's lungs and chest burned. The air was quickly being replaced with a hideous gas.

A bass rumble deep within the rakeworm preceded its next attempt to suck the barbarians closer to the stomach. Marigold found himself sliding up past boots, legs, torsos, heads, pushed himself through a moist cape. No movement. Cultist had probably died of nothing more than simple terror before he was dragged even this far up. But why was he still here? Why did this prick get to hang tight while the rest of them were being pulled deeper?

Another pair of boots hit Marigold's head. "Fucksh shake."

More convulsions. A deep groan throbbed from all sides. The throat tightened. For as wide as this fat fucking maggot was, there really wasn't much space in here.

"Radsh, we go' a bwockage."

A string of mumbled curses filtered up from below. As brave as Magnus was, Marigold could forgive him his panic. Haggar was probably thinking the same too.

As the worm's rumbling and griping began to dampen, Marigold heard something unexpected. A voice. A frantic and anxious voice.

"No! No! You can have these bastards instead, so you can. Go on, take it, ta- No! Off! Get off me!"

That was the fucking woodcutter alright.

"Rawage!" Marigold bellowed, lungs burning with the rancid remnants of the air he inhaled for it.

"Marigold?! Faster! There's some... some hole here! It's sucking me and everything in, so it is. I cannae hold it off, I'm running out of fucking cultists, so I am!"

"Cuwing uf."

"What?"

Marigold sighed and clamped his mouth shut again. That entrance was the stomach. Had to be. Magnus and Haggar had grasped the idea and were forcing themselves upwards once again. Marigold used his bruised and slimed head to squeeze and slide his way between the build-up of terrified, dying, or dead cultists. Fingers grappled, cries seeped out, despair filled the tunnel. Marigold's elbows saw to the ones that still breathed.

"Rawage!" he called.

"Here!" Ramage shouted from directly ahead, though he couldn't be seen. "Here, Marigold!" he yelled, amidst the incoherent babbles of stricken men who had never expected to find themselves this side of the lips of their 'Lord'.

The throat was at maximum capacity. Didn't the thing bloody choke? Maybe that was its problem, the worm was certainly raging. Trembles shook the beast. The throat contracted, pushing everyone together. Squeezing, crushing. A squelching and slurping noise opened up above, and hot, burning liquid gushed over Marigold's chest. This was it.

"Mag, Hag, uf!" Marigold screamed with a gasp of the toxic air. "Shar' cu'ing, now! Now!"

Hands found Marigold's shoulders as Magnus and Haggar began grunting with the effort of attacking the monster's oesophagus.

"Marigold?" came the woodcutter's wobbly voice.

"Yesh. Rook, man, poishon in keef, kake i', frow i' uf ingkoo shomach."

For a wonder, Ramage seemed to have translated every word perfectly, and a set of exploratory fingers began groping over Marigold's face, prodding him in the eyes and nose before they found his slobbering mouth and Nina's moist package of poison. It was a fucking relief to have that out, regardless of the rest of the situation; it was very unlikely it had been cleaned since its last stowage.

"Fuck!" Ramage bellowed, amidst the sucking and gurgling above. "It's in, Marigold. Me fucking hand. Fuck, it's burning so it is."

"Good man. Now, you've got two hands so stop your whinging about the one of them hurting. What are you? Five years old? Mag, Hag, can we go down?"

"Nope, fucking thing's closing up," screamed Magnus, "pushing us your way. It's up all the way."

"Up's death," Marigold called back plainly. "If we can't go down, we go to the side. Everyone! Cut! Stab! Use your fucking teeth and nails if you have to, we're getting out of here! Ramage, grab my chains, my wrists, I'm not going to be able to get you back if we lose you again." Marigold sent his bound hands up, felt the woodcutter grab tightly. With all of the strength he could muster, Marigold dragged the slime-caked local down between his legs, like some kind of vile, reverse birth. He used his feet to kick the man further. Maybe he kicked somewhat harder than was necessary, but Ramage wasn't going to complain when the alternative was death. Marigold, free of the man, fumbled around his belt to retrieve the knife he had stowed there. Almost dropped the slippery bastard, but then up he stabbed, taking an already dead cultist in the throat but it was good to finally get some purchase. "Fucking pricks, shove them up! Shove all of them up! Choke the cunt!"

"It's not fucking working, Chief!" Magnus wailed from deeper down. "The stabbing. Wall's too thick for it!"

"It fucking will work if we keep at it, man! It's a pissing worm! It's just flesh! No bone, no armour!" Fuck's sake it hurt to shout, his lungs burned at the top. Was this even air he was breathing anymore?

A deafening roar, like a blast from a colossal trumpet, tore through the throat. Wet wind forced its way down through the worm, over Marigold, Ramage, Magnus, and Haggar. The power of the blast forced the men down, further from the stomach entrance, thank Greldin, though scorching juices bathed all. Marigold clamped his eyes shut; he couldn't fucking see anything in here anyway.

"Cut! Fucking cut!" But Marigold now found for himself that it truly was of no use. The throat was soft and squishy, but still remained as tough as the steel his clan forged weapons with. He thrust his knife again and again, but it just slid to the sides. The shitting wall before him just would not yield.

The worm shuddered violently. An almighty quaking rippled down, almost shaking the weapon from Marigold's fingers. A new sound came from further within. A bark? Was that the once steady thud of the rakeworm's heartbeat beginning to falter? Faster. Slower. Harder. The poison was taking hold. Greldin's teeth, that *was* working quickly. Nina was right.

For the briefest of moments, the muscle wall of the throat relaxed.

Marigold thrust his tiny, shitty dagger into the flesh once again.

A spray of something hot and wet gushed over Marigold's face. It didn't burn but it tasted like fucking dirt. It was blood. It was beautiful, spurting worm blood! "Everyone, stab! Now!" he yelled frantically. "I've cut it! I've sliced the fucking thing open, keep at it! The fucker's giving up!"

Cries of exertion tinged with hope filled the vertical shaft as each man took steel and tooth and nail to the walls around them.

The worm wailed. The worm wobbled. The column shook. The small wounds tore.

Marigold let himself slide through the ragged slash he had opened up, prising it wider with his shoulders. Ramage followed, clinging once again to Marigold's chains for dear life. Well, it still remained to be seen if life could continue in this direction. Limbs thrashed, skulls cracked into one another. Anger. Confusion. Darkness. Hot, wet flesh slurped everywhere around them. A world without purchase. The chief hung there within the slimy, stinking fat of the worm. Must be how a fly felt in a fucking web. Or a man in a roughskin's pot. There wasn't going to be any breathing in here, let alone coordinated movement. His chains pulled taut before slackening, and in the dim, red gloom, Marigold saw the blurred outline of Haggar flop into this new circle of hell. Now what?

Fuck.

With his hands clasped tightly together, Marigold could barely move. He wanted to be away from the throat, but dying in the fat of the worm was going to be just as embarrassing as melting in its gut. By fucking Greldin, this was going from bad to bastard worse. Magnus arrived at the gash.

"What we doin' in here, Chief?" he panted. "Fucking worm's got a blue case around it, hasn't it? And fuck knows what else before that."

Fuck.

Marigold mumbled something back that was meant to be '*I don't fucking know*'. It was pissing hard to think when all of the available routes ended in death.

And then, abruptly, up was no longer up.

Marigold sloshed through the viscera and fat. Up, down, to the sides; he doubted even Greldin knew what was happening to them now. His chains dragged the others around with him, knotting them up in an awkward ball. The accompanying sounds were atrocious, and they were right in his fucking ears. Moaning, wailing, cracking, tearing, swilling. It was like the breaking of ice if you were under the water, but without the joy of knowing there was air above the ice. Much of it seemed to be from Ramage. The chaos, whatever the rest of it was, was ended with a demonic thud so deep and heavy it felt like it might stop Marigold's heart along with it. The tossing and turning halted, followed up with a sickly ripping that brought a dull blue glow with it, lighting the flesh around the chained men.

"Hole in the bastard!" Magnus screeched, sounding like he was everywhere at once. "Fucking hole in the bastard!"

Marigold twisted within the jelly of the fat and flesh to find that Magnus was indeed correct. The colossal maggot must have torn free of its cocoon and gashed itself open in the process. There was no time for more words, Marigold wasn't even sure where Magnus had found the breath to yell, but he certainly wouldn't be finding another lungful in here. Drowning in simple water was bad enough, inhaling this...

No. None of them were going to drown in the fat of a fucking worm. None of them. Marigold began twirling his arms, grabbing at anything that let him pull. Strings of sinew, thicker chunks of fat. The others followed suit, furiously cutting a swathe through the oily innards of the beast. A slight current pulled them all along as the guts began to pour outwards. The tear drew closer and Marigold licked his lips in a moment of forgetting what he was in. He gagged. The blue glow winked black, things running by outside in both directions. The sounds of the cult's cave hideout overtook that of the worm's swirling innards. The cries became defined as panic. Horror. A faction undone.

"On me! To me!"

"Where's Cecil? Have we found Lennan?"

"Has The Roof come out?!"

"Not that way! No!"

"Watch out, it's coming down there, too!"

A job well done, Marigold decided, whatever it was that happened next.

Marigold shoved his flesh-soaked head out into the relative cool of the cavern. Air. Clear air. They were right next to the dark and jagged rock of a cliff wall. Fucker must have split itself right open on that during the fall. Impossible to imagine how much weight had to be behind a collision of that magnitude. He tried not to think about the possibility of the mountain collapsing over them. Something glinted below, shone in the pale light of the Cerulean Hair on the walls.

It couldn't be?

Sear! His lost blade! There she bloody-well was, stuck there point down in the dirt and blood. Marigold struggled desperately, wriggling to stick his neck further out. The cliff above must have been where Pettar's last fight took place. The damn boy had better still be sat there in one piece. The blackened tail tip of worm bent away from the cliff – it appeared – back towards the shattered cocoon. Time to get out of this creature once and for all. He looked back at Sear. What a stroke of good fucking luck. What a welcome fucking sight.

Teeth gripped tightly onto the rough, yet waxy edges. The skin of the worm; almost too thick to latch onto. He bit hard and pulled. Again. Again. Out he slopped, out onto a mixture of wet sand and orange gore. There was a very obvious rushing sound coming from somewhere. Innards? Water? Difficult to tell. He slipped and slid as he pushed himself to his knees, smeared gooey hair from his eyes and face, and dug a foot deep into the ground so that he could anchor a hard tug on the chain. Ramage was birthed next from the wall of milky-white flesh, followed by Haggar and Magnus. They all spilled out on a cascade of fat and slime, Haggar's eyes were wide, white, bewildered.

"Fuck me, Chief," Magnus moaned. "Seemed like a good idea at the…"

Ramage, arse to the deck and half-submerged in the liquid mass, looked clearly hurt at where Magnus was going with that. It was obvious even with the thick coating of worm on his face.

"…I mean, good we got the woodcutter back, but let's not do it again, eh?"

"Fortunately," Marigold panted, "that was the last worm in here, Mag, and I'm certainly not planning on finding another."

The booming heartbeat of the monster cried out louder in the cavern, batted back and forth between the walls in infinite echoes. Spitertind must have been quaking in her roots from the outside. What were the folk of Elsdale thinking? Had they dared to run yet? Hard, soft, lighter, fainter, further apart. Erratic. The hitherto ceaseless pounding of the colossal organ faltered once more. A bang like a clap of thunder followed and a hiss and a groan seemed to seep from everywhere at once.

Dead.

Good.

This rakeworm was easily the greatest creature that Marigold had ever had a hand in killing. Made a fucking gargunnoch look like a mouse. By Greldin's fucking arse, it made some of the wizard towers he had climbed seem like mere huts. He doubted that anything would ever match the grandeur of this kill. Well, perhaps grandeur was the wrong word. It was, after all, just an oversized worm. Effort, then. The barbarian certainly hoped that this would mark the first and last time he took something down whilst being inside it. Too bad much of the victory went to Ramage and his delivery of the poison.

Marigold spat a shred of rancid flesh from his mouth with disgust and looked to his cold knees. Wet. Water was rising, and it certainly hadn't been there a moment ago.

"The fuck's all thi-"

"About to ask the same myself," Marigold interrupted Magnus.

There was a great deal of pulp from the worm, but it was obviously being swiftly diluted by a hidden source of rushing water. Hard to hear where that might be leaking from amidst the anguish of the remaining cult, but it had to be somewhere behind the hulking mass of the dead worm. Marigold traced the gargantuan corpse as it wound and bent up, along the walls of rock within the cavern. The sickly white flesh of the rakeworm was ripped and torn in countless places, leaking orange fluid from a myriad of gashes where it had grated its own flesh against the stone. Black flecks dotted the carcass like scabs, huddled together in patches. One of the flecks dropped off from high up. Those bloody tick things, no wonder they were so big.

The flabby beast had packed itself tightly into the rough cavern wall, over the spindly path that had brought them down here. Must have hit with some force, and it must have been in agony, if such creatures felt that sensation. It had certainly felt panic, judging by the noise it had made. Out of its blue casing, the monstrous bastard looked even larger. Gross. Impossibly long.

"So that's the way out fucked, eh?" He grumbled, turning away from the crushed track.

Magnus agreed with a nod and a cough. "Might be," he said. "But what a sight, Chief. Look at the fucking thing. We've gone and killed that. Doubt any of the others'll believe us though, doubt we can drag the bastard out to prove it, though I bet the stink'll soon back us up. Can y'imagine Vik's face when we tell him what we dropped?"

"Well, as much as I'd *like* to claim it, we're going to have to give Ramage the credit here," Marigold barely hid the grimace. "He threw the poison in, got a little burn on his hand for it. That there's your battle scar, Ramage." Marigold took in the dead monstrosity once again. The greatest creature he had ever *had a hand in killing*. Another bastard victory stolen from him today. Between a non-existent wizard, a simpleton that thought he could breathe water, and that slippery Lennan, the worm was just another tick to mark down on the list.

A snap and a slosh came from Haggar. The mute's fingers were wrapped tightly around the neck of an unfortunate cultist. Whoever thought that trying to sneak past three barbarians and a woodcutter was something approaching a decent idea deserved the attack. A dull pop sounded in the faceless man's throat as the windpipe was bent in on itself. Haggar slung the gurgling body down by Ramage.

"Let's get these pissing chains off, eh?" Marigold said, leading the joined men over to the hilt of his claymore, barely all that remained poking over the surface of the flood. "Can you fucking believe it?" he said, gripping Sear's hilt and yanking her free. "Thought I'd lost her for good, and here she was, waiting for me like the fine woman she is."

Haggar proffered his wrists and Marigold swung Sear through the chains like they were dry twigs, the mute then returned the favour for his chief. Ramage sloshed about along the line. "We'll have to sort the shackles out later," Marigold stated, as he freed Magnus from his bonds, "though they might actually be decent for smashing into the jaws of- Ramage!" he bit off. "What the fuck do you think you're doing?"

"I'm bloody freezing, so I am!" Ramage replied as he wound the sodden cloak of Haggar's discarded cultist corpse over his shoulders.

"You'll have that blue scrap of shit off you right now, or you'll be getting punched, stabbed, or both by me on our way out!"

"But they took my-"

"I'm not having you dress like one of them, and that's final. Here," Marigold said, tossing the dead man's thin sword over to the woodcutter. "You'll have one of their weapons and nothing more. A bit of fighting'll warm you right up. I know you prefer an axe, but metal's metal right now."

"Right, right you are," he grumbled.

"Good."

"Marigold?"

"Yes, Ramage?"

"Thanks for coming back for me. The second that thing grabbed me, I, I-"

"Ramage, you're no barbarian, but we couldn't just leave you, eh?"

"Nah, Ramage, you're a decent enough fella," Magnus said, "Just gotta grow those stones out a bit. They're a couple'a pebbles right now, but you'll get your rocks. Look what you've just made it through. You're the first man of Elsdale to make it out of that cunt, and the only one to drop it." He slapped a wide palm on the wall of white flesh that filled the hollow mountain. The smack echoed as the flesh beneath rippled gently at the source.

Ramage nodded gravely.

"Here, Chief, reckon that cocoon's worth anything?" He tapped a shred of it that reached up out of the water. "It's hard, real hard. Like stone." He knelt down to it. "Bends a bit. You want some?"

"Uh, I don't know. Can you break it off?"

Magnus heaved. "Don't think so, Chief."

"Then no, bloody well leave it! Maybe when it's all done you can come back with a saw."

"Fine, fine. We gonna get out of here, then?" Magnus asked the group, looking up at the ruined cliff as he groped his chin. "Gotta be some other way out of here, not seeing or hearing even half as many of those cult pricks as there were before. Either they've all been flattened, or they've another way out."

Marigold noted the water slapping at Magnus's thighs. It was rising fast, wherever it was coming from, and with no clues yet as to how much more there would be. The worm must have torn open a fissure into an underground river or something in its fall. "Aye, and let's make sure we drown as many of these bastards as we can on the way. Well, after we've had directions from one of them."

"Plan."

Marigold felt a tight grip on his shoulder. Expecting another cult member, he whirled around and blinked into Haggar's face. "What's wrong, Hag?" He wiped a globule of fetid worm gut from his around an eye.

Haggar was shaking his head, eyes wide. Pointing back across the only corner of the cavern that wasn't covered with rakeworm carcass. Dark blue shapes of fleeing cultists sped across the distant end of the cave.

"Great stuff, Hag, that'll be the way out, then. There're a few of them down there, eh? A pleasant little mop up job for us." Marigold swung Sear proudly.

Haggar shook his head again. He opened his empty mouth and hissed. He bit down on his bottom lip and furrowed his brow. The mute's eyes lit up. He made circular motions over his chest.

"What? What are you on about?"

Haggar changed tack. He stuck out a forefinger, then thrust it quickly between a circle made by thumb and forefinger on the other hand, grinning all the while.

"Wha- Nina?"

Haggar nodded quickly and happily.

"For fuck's sake, Haggar," Marigold and Magnus said in unison. "I don't think you're her type, but you're right," continued Marigold, "Greldin knows she stopped us from being worm food. He'd want her out for that." He puffed air through his lips. They were dangerously close to becoming full heroes for the people of Elsdale. He had just wanted to be able to go hunting without some caped pricks sneaking up behind him in the woods, and here they were, saving the damn land. Acting for a good greater than that of the clan. "Come on. We'll go and bloody get her."

Ramage took the first tentative steps into the gloomy flood in nothing more than his tattered underclothes, his scavenged sword clutched tightly.

Marigold watched the man with a small degree of pride. "Well, well, well, Ramage, on you go. Lead the way.

You'll have those rocks before we're even out of this pissing cavern."

Chapter Nine

WASH OUT

Anybody could have told Marigold that he and his men had stumbled out of the worm and into the Pits themselves, and he'd have damn well believed them. Yells of fear rode the air, mingled with the distinct crumbling of compromised rock, while the biggest carcass he had ever seen lay gracelessly behind. Ramage, Haggar, and Magnus sloshed ahead, wading through rising water that was now well over thigh-deep and flecked with strings of orange gore and assorted floating rammel. The group snaked between jagged spires of natural rock formations, beneath the blue glow of the moss-covered cavern walls. Marigold, now using Sear as a guide in the murky flood, couldn't help but try and focus on the distant screams and wails of horror and despair that seemed to ooze from everywhere at once. Above, behind, ahead. No origin to determine. Hell all around. Not even the vast, pallid carcass did anything to dampen the cries in this fucking echo chamber. A world of despair. As knees parted the water, bodies and floating remains of broken furniture drifted on by. Marigold gave another glance to the cadaver of the beast. They'd put a fair amount of distance between it and the rocky walls of Mt. Spitertind's interior, and he had a fine view of the entirety of the creature. Perhaps it was simply the cocoon that had made it appear to be a particularly thick column, but in its death throes the worm had managed to stretch out and perfectly divide the floor of the enormous cavern in two, and yet still it reached up high. The mountain was massive and the hollow was deep, yet the great, dead rakeworm was close on twice the length it had been before slopping gracelessly from the side of its cocoon. A true colossus. What remained of its shell was a tattered and pale rag hanging from the stalactites high above and no doubt flattened beneath the worm below. Creaks and groans joined the human cacophony. Whether these were the noises of a dying beast still settling into place at the bottom of the mountain or the herald of something far worse, Marigold could not be sure. All he knew was that he wanted out of this damn hellhole, and the sooner that happened, the better.

"Hey, Ramage," barked Magnus, pointing at something floating just ahead. "There's that useless fucking crossbow of yours."

"That is *not* useless, absolutely not!" Ramage sounded quite hurt. The indignant woodcutter broke away, splashing through the swirling shit to reclaim his beloved weapon. "I got that bleedin' priest between the teeth with this, so I did," Ramage said proudly, holding the dripping crossbow aloft like it was a storied weapon of ancient legend. Damn thing still had some bolts attached to the stock, for fuck's sake.

"And did it kill him?" Marigold asked, chewing a splinter of something sharp out of the side of his thumb.

"Well, no. It didn't. But did you see the look on his face?"

"Aye, I did. And at the time I thought you'd *meant* to miss," said Marigold.

Haggar rasped a painful laugh, but his grin seemed genuine. Ramage's head dropped.

"Just aim up a bit next time, eh? Or down," Magnus added. "Now then, Haggar, where to next?"

Before Ramage could rejoin the short line, Haggar had waded to the front, jabbing furiously at a dark opening in the cavern wall ahead and to the left. A hole that two cultists were fleeing from at that moment.

"Oh aye, Haggar, you think if you get there first it'll be your cock in her mouth when we're all out?" Magnus had a penchant for stating what never needed to be said.

Marigold shook his head. Tongue or no tongue, the man hadn't lost his lecherous nature in those flames.

A strong wave surged and pushed Marigold forward. He jabbed Sear into the sand to steady himself and looked back. Most of the wall torches in the cavern had been lost when the life had faded from the rakeworm, but the Cerulean Hair on the distant walls drew more than enough attention to a cascade of billowing white foam from behind the mouth end of the bastard maggot. The crashing and rushing soon drowned out the moans of the cultists that still remained within. Either a lot had died, or a lot had escaped. The latter wasn't going to be good for Elsdale.

"Ain't got much time, Chief," Magnus yelled amidst the growing din.

"Well aware of that, Mag." True enough, the water was a genuine concern, but just as his friend had stated the obvious Marigold had caught a flash of white and blue peeking out from behind one of the large stalagmites that littered the cavern floor like unruly teeth.

"Hag, Mag, Ramage, get a fucking move on and get that woman out. If you see any more of the cunts in the capes you shout. We regroup, and we follow them, understood? We can kill any escapees outside, but we need to know where the rats are all escaping to first. I'll catch you up if you're not out before. We'll have a fight on our hands."

Magnus lunged through the water to catch up with Ramage and Haggar. "And where the fuck're you off, Chief?" he called back.

"Maybe nowhere, I'll find out in a moment. Grab a handful of that moss, or one of the torches on the walls if they haven't all gone out by the time you're there. Dark in that tunnel, remember? You'll want to see what's coming. Listen for clicking."

"Right you are, Chief." His friend nodded before putting his hands to his mouth and yelling. "Hag! Ramage! Hold on!"

Marigold let the splashing trio get a fair distance away before he began quietly shuffling through the flood to the suspect rock formation. Water just about up to his damn stones now. Soon it would be tickling them, but this glimpse of white and blue really was of more interest at the moment. If he was right – and he usually was – that cloth he had spied being snatched from view belonged to Lennan. Now, for sure that sack of old bones had heard him, but unless he had managed to swim silently away from this rock, the old bastard was still hiding there. Marigold kept very still, glaring intently, scouring the black edges for any sign of movement.

A flash of pointed flesh. A nose!

Marigold sped through the water like Sear through skin. Within the blink of an eye he was on the other side of the natural pillar.

"Got you, you dusty fucker!" Marigold snatched his quarry by the throat with his free hand.

Sure enough, this was Lennan, albeit without his ridiculous hat. He seemed rather short minus that fashion statement. What a stroke of luck this was. The old shit wouldn't be dodging the afterlife for much longer. Lennan squirmed and wheezed under Marigold's grip, though truth be told the barbarian wasn't holding that tightly. Yet. Skinny arms dropped feeble fists onto Marigold's shoulders and arms. A light pattering.

This was too easy, but it didn't feel wrong.

He wanted to savour this a little, especially after the full day of disappointment he'd had. He cast the robed leader to the water, temporarily losing him beneath the murky surface. After a moment of wondering whether or not he had already actually drowned the shithead, Lennan emerged, coughing and spluttering, spouting mouthfuls of the filthy, gore-stained water.

"Y-you're alive! How?" Lennan swallowed loudly, spat out another mouthful, "W-wh-what are you going to do?"

"Of course I'm fucking alive, who do you think I am? And, because I'm *still* alive, I now get the chance to put an end to your miserable existence." Marigold strode forwards, an iron giant before the crumpled figure below. "How else did you think any of this was going to end?"

Lennan stumbled up and tripped back down, lost himself beneath the surface once again. Was he going to voluntarily end himself? No. Back he came, scrambling up and onto his feet. The last strands of his lank, grey hair clung to his face. His sodden robes highlighted just how frail and malnourished the man really was. His eyes were wide and white, pupils nothing more than wobbling pin-pricks. His jaw shuddered. Cold, fear... Probably both.

"Now," Marigold said, "how do we do this? Sear really doesn't mind which way she enters; she's no prude. I could leave it up to you, but I've a strong suspicion you'll take a while to settle on an answer, am I right?"

The splashing continued as Lennan's thrashing limbs failed to put any meaningful distance between hunter and prey.

"Neck is too easy. Too quick. Same goes for slicing through your middle." Marigold swung Sear menacingly, acting out in the air the various cuts he was mulling over. "I could light her up, but that would be a fucking waste seeing as though you'd just put yourself out when you dropped beneath the water for the last time."

"I'm nothing to you! Nothing!" The priest's ancient vocal chords strained. "What difference does it make if you kill me? Our Lord is dead, all was for nothing," he wept as his eyes fell upon the fleshy corpse.

"That's right, your worm is dead. So, what use are you now to anyone? To anything?"

"I'm nothing now, nothing! You know it, I know it. Let me die in peace, I'm not long for this world. I-i-it's my men you should be chasing down, they'll already be slaughtering anybody left in Elsdale. Why don't you try and save them before there's nothing left to save?" Lennan firmed himself up, arms fixed rigidly by his sides in some final act of defiance. "What do you fucking want with me?"

"To spill your guts, perhaps?" Marigold ignored the man's pleas. "You could watch them as the current tries to tug them away." Marigold chuckled quietly to himself. "It appears that I'm just as indecisive as-"

The discs of black came out of nowhere. They shot at Lennan's sides, front, and back like striking snakes. Shield-sized bodies, clicking wildly. Tiny legs wriggling in ecstasy as mandibles struck flesh and bone. Tearing, cracking, slurping. Heads buried themselves deep, in Lennan's ribs, chest, back, mouth. The feast began, and Sear wasn't invited.

"Fuck!" Marigold howled in dismay.

Lennan teetered on weak legs, arms shaking wildly as he was unable to fall in any direction. The weight of each giant tick balanced him perfectly. A groan came from beneath the creatures, the last sound that would ever leave Lennan.

Marigold staggered back, suddenly very aware of his own exposed chest. Ramage didn't need that flimsy cape he'd wanted so much, he needed a shitting breastplate. They all did.

As the ticks filled themselves, Lennan finally fell back. With a splash, he disappeared into the murky water. The arse-end of the mouth-sucking creature broke the surface, shaking slightly as it drank. Bloody bubbles rose and burst.

"I don't fucking believe it," Marigold seethed. Victory snatched from his grasp once again. He held Sear up, over the suspected resting place of the damned priest. He could stab down, he probably wasn't quite dead just yet. But...

There was just no point.

The damage was done. The ticks had won this one. No tower, no wizard, The Roof voluntarily drowning himself, Ramage delivering the poison, and now a gang of fucking insects had taken the final scraps of glory left on this cursed trip. He hadn't even seen the little cunts coming. He assumed they could swim. Marigold looked at the water, then up into the abyss overhead. How far had they leapt from to maintain that level of accuracy?

Marigold held Sear firmly, over his chest. Whether he was being watched or not, he felt eyes on him. What about his back? What if they were eyeing up his sides? He wasn't going to be able to protect his back if they mounted a rear attack, but he might slice one if it came at his front. With one final glare at bubbles by his legs, Marigold edged back through the water, twisting round and round in his search for ticks, dizzying himself he twisted so quickly. Melting in a worm was bad, being drained by a mindless insect was even higher up the scale. The sooner he found a way out of this hellhole, the fucking better.

"For fuck's sake!" cried Magnus

Marigold heard the man long before he saw him. Heard him repeat that same line again and again. Heard the giant bastard straining and moaning ahead as he lunged through the tunnel to meet his men at the cells. The low roof made the threat of drowning soon seem all the more realistic to entertain. His cock and stones were entirely submerged now; the tunnel evenly split between air and water. Moving with any sense of speed was not easy, and the threat of scraping his skull on the rocks above was a constant worry.

"Fucking gate, fucking shitty sword. Haggar, pull! Ramage, chuck that fucking crossbow away and get both hands on the bastard. Heave! Greldin's teeth, fucking heave, it's only a fucking gate."

"Magnus," Nina's calm voice said. "How about if you-"

"It's no fucking use, love, it won't budge."

"What about if we-"

"Ramage, we've been at that same bit since we came in, it's not fucking happenin'"

Magnus was not having a good time facing defeat at the bars of an inanimate object.

"Right. Just go," Nina shouted. "Get out of here while you've still time! Appreciate the attempt but I never thought I'd be getting out of here anyway."

The sound of flesh and bone on metal was clear, even over the splashing water and echoes swirling in from the central cavern.

"Hag, it's no use, it ain't gonna work!"

"Greldin fucking wept," yelled Marigold, as he sloshed into the open cell space. The top of the bars had a ball of Cerulean Hair stuffed between them, a makeshift light source for the dingy prison. All of his men were clamouring around the locked cell gate, scratching heads, stroking beards. "Out of the way, all of you." He yanked Haggar away from the rusted bars. The mute splashed back onto his arse, water lapping at his chin as he glared at Marigold. What the fuck? He was mute, not deaf. "For fuck's sake, you're all bloody useless. You can pull steel apart just about as well you can breathe fire, Haggar, so I've no idea why you were bothering to try that." With one smooth motion, Marigold slid Sear directly through the bolted section of the gate. The door lunged inwards with a rusty squeal as filthy water frothed between the bars. "Simple as that, you fucking clowns. Nina, the worm's dead, the cult's fucked. Out you come." He offered an arm but it wasn't taken. Her sodden rags were clutched about her waist, sliding off bony shoulders under the sheer waterlogged weight of it. She was so short that the water was lapping at her tits. "Honestly, how many pissing men does it take to get a girl out of a cage?"

Magnus tapped a finger at each man in turn. "Looks like four, Chief," he said, looking puzzled.

"Didn't think to try any of those blades you picked up?"

"All broke, Chief. Snapped on the first try, each of them. Besides, where've you been?"

"Thought I'd seen Lennan but it was just another disappointment," Marigold evaded. He didn't want to have to regale them all with news of yet another failure today.

"Nah, Chief, old bastard won't have made it through that, not with the worm coming down," Magnus said confidently, offering a hand to help Nina through the water. "An' even if he did, he'd be lying underwater, nursing a broken hip while his last lungful gave out." Nina took *his* hand.

"You're probably right," Marigold agreed as he stepped back to let the pair through. Whatever really had happened back there, Lennan was dead regardless. He should probably just be happy about that.

"So, are we going to stand around here discussing dead men until the water reaches our necks?" Nina spat, pushing an advancing Haggar away from her side. A look of utter bewilderment painted her face as she watched the water rise around the Chief and his men. "You avoided the worm's stomach but you're all happy to wait around and drown in plain old water here?"

"There's bits of worm in the water, here, you seen?" Magnus added – unhelpfully – as he scooped up a palmful and let dark strings dangle down between his fingers.

Marigold rolled his eyes and batted Magnus's hand down. Nina was right to complain, of course, but how in the Pits were they actually going to get out of here now? "The way up and out is gone, Nina. We had been trying to find some cultists to follow out, but they all seem to have escaped."

"Up and out?"

"Aye, same way as we came in."

"You didn't come in through the river caves?"

"What river caves?" Marigold scowled at the woodcutter. "Ramage? What river caves?"

"I didn't-"

"Augh, just follow me, all of you." Nina gathered her drenched and ill-fitting fabric around her chest and began striding alone into the tunnel.

"You'll want to watch out for the ticks, Nina. You won't see them coming," Marigold called ahead, ushering the men after her.

"You just worry about yourselves, I'll be fine," Nina snapped.

"You sure we did the right thing here, Haggar?" Marigold whispered to the mute.

Haggar gave a stern, sideways glance. There would have to be a spectacular turn around in his fortunes now for him to end up with the reward he had seemingly been expecting for the rescue.

"You really bloody did it," Nina said, gazing upon the pale, dead rakeworm in awe. "You'll have to tell me how you managed that when we're out and safe."

"Just where is it that's safe, then?" Marigold asked. "With all this water rising, everywhere's starting to look the same." His stones weren't just being tickled, they were being fucking drowned. His nipples weren't far off now either. Nina wasn't long for losing her shoulders beneath the surface. Nor was Ramage for that matter. He wasn't a tall man.

"Just let me get my bearings," she said, irritably. Maybe it was being cooped up for so long, but for a rescued person she was remarkably tetchy. "Worm's over The Table, your way in is up there – and ruined – so the way out must be over... there!" She jabbed a finger towards a large black spot on the dim, blue wall ahead. "It's a cave. Looks like the other holes but notable for its size. Its quite obvious size, in my opinion. The river cave outside isn't much smaller."

"Ramage, we're having words about this when we're out," Marigold said plainly. "Nina's not even a local and she knows this place better than you fucking do." The black spot was only a short wade away. All of those holes that Marigold had studied upon their arrival in this pit and one of them was a way in and out of the bloody place. Fucking typical. The church on the top was clearly intended as a ruse for anyone daring to venture up while doubling as a rite of passage for the condemned taken from the town. A grander way to meet an end than traipsing through sodden tunnels: up to the heavens, then down into the Pits. Even so, the river tunnels explained how the cult were able to appear before potential escapees from the town.

Thud.

"D'arrgh," Ramage choked as he pulled himself up out of the water. "What the fuck was that? Marigold? What was it?"

"I don't pissing know, do I? Like I've said a few times now, *you* were supposed to be the expert around here!"

"Marigold, I'm sorry, so I-"

Thud. Thud.

"The worm!" Nina warned. "You've not killed it yet."

Marigold stumbled beneath the force of the next beat to see a spasm ripple the flesh of the worm from tip to tail. Only his own death was going to make this day any worse, and right now that seemed fairly imminent. At the very least it would mean an end to this nonsense.

Thud. Thud. Thud.

The drumming came quickly, the quaking shook the non-carcass.

Thud. Thud. Thud. Thud. Thud. Thud.

Then silence.

Marigold looked at Haggar. He was still staring at Nina with moons-eyes. Ramage shuffled close to Magnus. Magnus shook his head at Marigold, eyes wide, brow furrowed.

"We need to make our way to the exit, now," she warned, already splashing on ahead. "I don't know what happens at this point. None of my order ever made it this far alive. Never heard reports of a worm coming back from that poison though, so this might be it finally giving in. Come on!"

"You heard her," yelled Marigold, "get your arses moving! Or do you want to end up inside that thing again?"

"You… you went in?" Nina looked horrified as she halted for a moment, eyeing up the worm.

"Hand feeding wasn't really an option."

Nina ran on.

Ramage was already ahead, showcasing the remnants of his cowardice as he sloshed through the water. Magnus and Haggar strode warily, eyes searching every direction at once. For his part, Marigold was concerned on three fronts: he didn't fancy drowning, being swallowed again, or becoming a feast for a tick.

Thud.

Louder and stronger than the last, the boom had an air of finality to it. The final pump of a heart fit to burst. The cave shook while the flood heaved. The group fled as fast as was possible through chest-high water. Abruptly, the water drew back. Ramage went down, floundering over the lowered surface. Haggar hauled him back up. Magnus scooped Nina into the air and flung her on his shoulders. She didn't complain.

Marigold watched uneasily as his stones received their first airing in some time. Where had the water gone?

Wearily, he followed the flow, which brought his eyes back to the rakeworm.

The monster arched up. A great rigid curve reaching into the jagged upper recesses of the cave. The flood dragged back, frothing and foaming and churning white where it crashed into the rest of the water that had been waiting behind the body.

Barely a heartbeat passed. The worm began to fall.

"Run! Marigold, everyone! Fucking run! We get out now or we don't get out at all!" Nina screamed. They were all already paces ahead.

Magnus was the farthest, Nina bobbing up and down, riding him like a rukh. The water no longer held him back now it was at his knees. Haggar was just behind, gripping an ashen Ramage by his hair.

"Into the cave! Quick! Quick!" the rescued woman was frantic. "Into the cave before all that comes back!"

The worm split down the middle as it hit the deck for the final time. The ground twisted savagely, almost knocking Marigold from his feet. A cascade of orange flesh and blood dyed the deluge that roared over the top of the rakeworm. The beast's innards leaked out into a furious tsunami of water, gore, and death. Marigold somehow turned a trip into a smooth roll and leapt right back up. He wasn't fucking drowning here today.

The rumbling water engulfed everything in its path, sickeningly powerful as it hurtled across the hollow. The wave grew, reared up, gathering violent momentum as it bore back down on the group.

The escape route was so close, but the death wave was closer.

White froth spat and hissed into Marigold's hair as he caught up with his friends. Marigold hadn't run this fast since fleeing the thrall of his childhood captor's some thirty winters ago, and he'd had the good fortune to be running alone. Here, alongside Magnus, Haggar, Ramage, and Nina...? All of them saw the fear etched on his face. Marigold feared very little, but drowning was very high on that small list of unacceptable ways to go.

Something hard slapped him across his back.

As he stumbled to his knees, a cut of broken table sailed on over the top of him. The flood swirled in around him, so strong he was swept clean off his feet and onto his arse. But before his backside could hit the sand and rock below the wave carried him up and thrust him right over the others. He clutched Sear like his life depended on it. He'd lost her once today, and it wasn't going to happen again, no matter how useless she was against the force of a flood. He smashed face first into the back of Haggar's knees, who had somehow ended up in front again. Haggar toppled, lost his grip on Ramage. The woodcutter was wrenched out of sight. Nothing but thundering water anywhere. Marigold caught snatches of faces, of mouths open and unable to yell. He saw Magnus hurled forwards just as he went fully under for the first time, Nina was no longer clinging onto him. A punch to the chest from the crashing water squeezed the air from his lungs, a mess of bubbles clouding anything he might have otherwise been able to see.

Air.

He gasped greedily. Hair flooded his eyes. Between the strands of ruined braid, the cavern wall was rushing towards them. Another head bobbed up. Nina.

She was mouthing something. 'Swim'? How the fuck could anyone swim in this? She was away, arms flailing. Something gripped Marigold's leg, and up came Haggar by his side, eyes pleading for deliverance. His tongueless mouth was agape, desperately sucking in air.

Haggar disappeared.

Where were the others?

Nina was ahead again. Amidst the shaking and swirling and thundering water, Marigold caught a glimpse of her arm prodding down at the water. The wall was close. Getting smashed against that was going to either instantly kill them or mortally wound them to the point where drowning would be the natural successor.

Drown against the wall or drown down below?

Not much of a fucking choice, it had to be said, especially after all that had come before. If Greldin was watching any of this today and favoured any of them at all, now was the time for him to show he could step in when he wanted to. Detached from his followers though the god was, he still wanted proud deaths for his clan. Just one of them, one of them had to make it out alive.

Marigold took a deep breath and plunged beneath the surface.

A blue-caped body rushed by him, dragged deeper by some current that Marigold wasn't yet embroiled in. He held Sear out like a rudder, clinging tightly to her hilt as her blade was battered with assorted rammel from the caves, bits of broken rock, more wrecked furniture, more bodies. They were being washed out. The cave exit had to be down there, in the murk. That's where this was all going.

But he couldn't see a damn thing.

Something bumped his back, twisted him around. Now he was being dragged backwards. A substantial weight cracked him in the shins and rolled him upside-down. Bubbles fled his lips. His lungs already began to burn, as though they had decided it was better to give it up now than drag out the inevitable any longer. Well, that was his decision to make, not theirs. Marigold twisted and spun in the water, unable to do anything other than accept the ride he was being taken on. It didn't matter how little he wanted to drown, the flood had other ideas.

Marigold's head crunched against something sharp and immoveable. Fuck it hurt. He almost spat out the last of his breath. Rock. His arms were shredded next. Then his side, his legs, his back. He was in the grinder. No floor, no walls, no ceiling, just all-encompassing pain and razor-sharp debris. The water was briefly tinged with red, before darkness claimed the remaining colour.

This whole trip really had been a stupid fucking idea. This would mark the last time he was making any big decisions on the back of an unknown fucking cask of ale, in an unknown fucking village, with an unknown fucking worm living inside a Pits-damned hollow mountain.

Seemed like that last time had been and gone whether he liked it or not.

Chapter Ten

BONY OLD BASTARD

It was wet cold that brought Marigold round to thinking straight again. Ice, all over, head to toe. His first thought was simply a compelling desire to fill empty and aching lungs. Fortunately for Marigold's continued existence, his muscles weren't feeling as spontaneous as his mind. His second thought was that something wasn't quite right.

Where in the Pits was he?

Marigold opened his eyes to the sodden chill. That hurt. Strands of blurred, yellow hair hung before his face, intertwined with twisted strings of blood and flecks of dirt as they were gently tugged on ahead amidst rippling light.

Light. Colour. Too much for him to be underground anymore; the moss hadn't been *that* bright. Either Greldin was offering him the celestial path or these were rays from the sun. A spasm of stinging pain in his back reminded him of the ordeal that had come before. He'd been… washed out of the cult's base of operations. But he wasn't being dragged along anymore. He was weightless. He was…

Still underwater. Still on the precipice of drowning.

That brought him fully to.

The warm shimmer of outside was tantalising close, even tangible within this freezing body of water. He flexed his fingers, immediately gripping tightly again with his right hand as he felt Sear's hilt slide across his palm. A fucking stroke of luck he still held her. Well, it would be if he managed to break the surface before these final dregs of air gave out. His arms were leaden, no longer his to control. Double leaden for the arm that held his beloved weapon. Rotten leaves, pine needles, clumps of grass and fine flecks of rock swirled around him on the gentle current. A fine joke to have him take the water in here, barely an arm's length from pissing safety. Must be how everyone who drowned felt. His death would be no less idiotic than that of The Roof's.

Sear anchored him. But if she drowned here, he drowned with her. The fire in his lungs substituted her flames, almost diluted the chill of the water. He glanced around slovenly, such an effort. The river or stream was narrow but deep. The bloated eyes of an unfortunate fellow bulged by Marigold's waist, while the rest of the body tottered lazily along the muddy bed. A fluffy black beard danced in the water, buoyed by large jowls that rose to join rounded cheeks. Well, if it wasn't the cunt that had kneed him in the eye back before the cells. His fat nose was even fatter now that it was full of water. Seemed about right that Death had found the man before Marigold managed to. Seemed about right that Death had left him there for Marigold to see. The fat man's light blue cape reached up to the surface in vain, shoulders higher than Marigold's hanging feet.

Time to get out of the water.

With an inhuman effort, Marigold swung his feet onto the pauldrons of the drowner and pushed down hard. His shoulders sputtered into adrenaline-soaked life. Up he went. His chest was ready to burst. Marigold had deep lungs, but he wasn't a member of the fucking Gillfolk. His chest spasmed, fighting the impulse to breathe in what became the most difficult fight he had ever faced. With a heave his sword arm broke out. Iced wind enveloped the hand that still clutched Sear. In an almighty show of strength, he flung her to what he hoped was a river bank. He pushed on the bloated man's head with one final act of defiance, kicking the cunt in the eye as he left him.

His lips finally felt air.

Marigold gasped like a dying man. His efforts to draw in as much air as was physically possible deteriorated into hoarse screeching that took not only him by surprise, but also startled a large, yellow-beaked eagle that had been peacefully tearing away at a fish from the roots of a tree by the river. The creature took off, beating its huge wings, brown and white. He or she – Marigold hadn't the wherewithal to check in his gasping – squawked in rage at its interrupted meal. Half of that meal fell from its talons, catching Marigold full in the face with a wet slap.

"For fuck's sake," he wheezed, as his aching arms grasped out for land, smearing the innards of the ruined fish from his face, scales and all.

Fingers dug deep into wet dirt and grass, compacting uncomfortably beneath his fingernails. The wind ate greedily into the wounds on his bare back as he dragged himself out of the water. Agony though it was, he'd have to weather the pain and the chill for now. There was Sear, glistening on the bank as the last drops of water flowed along her grooves and dripped back into the river. He wiped another round of fish scales from his tongue.

Whether he could believe it or not, he was out. Alive. Alone.

Where was everyone else?

Against the agonising spasms from his neck and spine, Marigold sat up on the bank, cross-legged. His goatskin trousers were a tattered mess, but at least his stones were still clothed and felt intact. A hand dragged over his forehead came away bright red. As his eyes left his palm, he caught sight of a gash in his bicep, and it really was his bicep: muscle lay shredded at the edge, skin ripped and peeled back. No wonder his arms hurt so fucking much. The pain in his back wasn't dissimilar and he was rather glad that those particular wounds were out of sight. The journey out of Spitertind had done a fair number on him, but that wasn't uncommon such excursions. *'Shredded is better than deaded,'* as Haggar had once said after a particularly violent battle with a bear. Well, he was mostly correct. Marigold was still intact, and that was the extent he was going to dwell on it. Some healing was due when he made it back to the clan but, thank Greldin, his body tended to rebuild itself quickly. He was alive, that was all that mattered.

The river by his feet ran between trees, which he hoped to be the same forest that surrounded Elsdale, and on the side situated below the south of the mountain. Yes, Marigold could hold his breath for a long time, but he couldn't be *too* far from where he started. Here, on the bank, the trees were sparse and he was glad of the faint warmth that broke through the canopy at this chill time of year. Crisp caps of snow coated circles of grass and lined roots here and there, but in the open sunlight it became a pale mist that rose up into the mixed leaves and needles of deciduous and coniferous origin. The peak of Spitertind loomed beyond, still there, still covered in thick snow. The worm may have fucked the insides of the mountain, but the exterior shell gave no hint as to the nightmare that had taken place within. How many other mountains had he walked in the shadows of, or climbed the peaks of, while remaining utterly ignorant of a growing rakeworm?

Marigold checked the river for anybody else that may have made it. His solitude was somewhat concerning. Either everyone was dead, or they had left him for dead. He agreed with himself that they couldn't really be blamed if the latter was the case. Being alive at this point was a fairly unexpected boon. No bodies was the most positive result Marigold could take from this.

But where was everyone else if they had made it? It wouldn't be the first time that Marigold had been the sole survivor of an expedition, but by Greldin's pearly fucking teeth, he hoped this wasn't another repeat of that. This was supposed to have been a simple trip to massacre a gods-damned cult. A basic job!

Marigold slumped back down. His tattered behind was glad of the crisp bite of frost within the grass. As the pain melted out in the haze of numbness, other senses began to pick up.

Namely, hearing.

Metal rung on metal from somewhere in a distance that remained directionless thanks to the thick woodland surrounding the battered barbarian. Ragged voices broke in, screaming orders, yelling curses, begging for mercy. Armoured feet pounded ice-hardened ground. Faint though the sounds were, battle was raging, and it couldn't be far.

"I-i-it's my men you should be chasing down, they'll already be slaughtering anybody left in Elsdale."

The Crystal fucking Cult. Or what was left of it. Enough to fight, and to be completely fair to Elsdale, it sounded like they had grown the stones to fight back at last.

Marigold threw a hand out to retrieve Sear and dragged himself up with her. Blood spattered to the grass as he shook himself free of the cold and pain like a worn-out dog. Both beard and hair braids had come entirely undone, slapping him across the neck and face. He cleared his eyes. The pain was still there, but all of that shit was temporary and could be blocked out if necessary. Pain was a luxury to dwell upon when the fighting was done. Meant you were still alive. Marigold pawed at the drenched belt around his waist. Sear's last remaining vial still hung there by some miracle. Unbroken, ready to slide into her hilt. The barbarian closed his eyes, breathed out, and listened.

It was all going on behind him.

He spun on the spot, kicking up grass and fallen needles. Marigold sprinted into the woods. Between densely packed firs he shoved. Brittle branches broke, twigs snapped, ice crunched. The sunlight of the riverside glade quickly faded, replaced by the suffocating natural walls that had trapped Elsdale with the cult for all these years. Wood splintered against the warrior's skin, bark became trapped within the blood that drenched him, Sear stripped grasping limbs from the trees with precision strikes. The forest conceded, Marigold was granted passage.

Splinters of light between trees became patches of sun, became visions of battle, became cries of pain and death.

Spitertind watched on as the showdown played out among the bloodied grass, mud, and patches of snow beneath her. The semicircle of firs and spruces and oaks ensured all involved would remain involved. The battlefield was a wide circle. One side full of metal and blue, the other side a compact wedge of brown-cloaked Elsdale folk hemmed in by their own empty housing. No escape for them. The town forces were few and obviously on the backfoot. More blue-cloaks emerged from narrow slits between the trees. A disappointingly large number of them. How many of the fuckers had even died back there? Had there been a company already stationed outside? An arrow tore past Marigold's face as he left the columns of the trees for the knee-high grasses of the village fields. It still rang in his ear as it buried itself loudly into a thick trunk behind him. Another came, striking Sear square in the blade with a ringing clang. A pale-faced local held the bow. Marigold could see the fellow shaking from here, the fellow who had been playing darts in the inn the other night.

"Watch where you're fucking shooting, you prick. I'm on your pissing side!" he yelled. Fucking ideal. Run all this way just to take a friendly arrow to the heart.

"Well, why are you over there?" he hissed. Your folk are all waiting down behind the houses for the ambush." The man nodded beyond the huddle of cloaks and drew another arrow, running off as he turned to face a new target across the field.

"My folk? Haggar? Magnus? Hey!" Marigold barked as he watched the third arrow fly, straight into a shield held high, snapped, and broke. No answer and a useless shot.

Where were his men?

Marigold crept carefully through the grass. The slices across his back had him twitching more than he was happy with. Even so, the mass of cloaks hadn't spotted him yet, though the possibility of one or two of the shits bursting out from behind had him on edge. A sea of blue capes twirled over gleaming metal. A hundred of the bastards? Two hundred? Marigold wasn't great with numbers, he just knew there were far more of them than there were Elsdale folk. A line of swords and shields pushed towards an uneven row of pitchforks and axes and shovels. Flames already leapt from the thatched rooftops behind the defenders. Weapons versus tools. Arrogance versus desperation. At this rate a slaughter was imminent.

A series of sharp, familiar whistles pierced the opening from multiple points in the woodland to the east. A single throwing axe rose high up into the sky, other the folk of Elsdale, seeming to hang for a moment over the enemy. Down it arced, fast, deadly. It buried itself square in the face of a cultist on the front of the line. Not an axe for wood, an axe for flesh! An axe of the clan! A halberd followed from elsewhere between the trees and an arm clutching a sword fell near Axe-Face.

"GRELDIN!" a chorus rang.

Marigold smiled grimly, quickening his pace towards the side he was fighting for. Oh, there was going to be a slaughter alright.

Men and women that Marigold knew well ruptured from between forest and town dwellings. The fighting folk of Elsdale parted to let them through. Shaved heads and topknots, arms as thick as the legs of most town folk, blue and red warpaint, screams of ecstasy, of bloodlust taking over. Flesh flashed between flapping skins, sweat glistened even as the cold breeze whipped long braids about.

The barbarians were here. Probably come to find their errant chief, though they'd simply appreciate the fight if nothing else.

Marigold roared as well, pounding into battle with Sear held high. He joined the farmers and woodcutters and barbarians at the edge of the fighting line as it gathered vicious momentum and pushed back into the cultists. The enemy forces hesitated for a moment, not expecting the trial that was rushing towards them. The clash, the resonation of metal on metal, metal through flesh, metal on bone. This was what Marigold lived for.

The crush began.

Someone's blood painted Marigold's face. Heat, wet, and blue fabric plastered itself over his chest. A body before him fell, couldn't tell if he'd been responsible for it but it made a step to launch himself from. Up he leapt, down he aimed. Sear opened up the fucker below him from the shoulder down. Blue-clad bodies toppled in over their split comrade. Feet slipped on gore and entrails. The grass had a new drink to try today. By his side, one of his kin beat a man with a severed leg, thrashing a helmet until it was far too dented to contain an intact head. Cries rose among the cloaked attackers, and not of the rallying sort. This was blind panic. The chaos of battle grew as seasoned barbarians hacked their way through the frontlines without a second thought for their own safety. Gallant, showy swordplay simply shattered against the sheer brutality of men who fought solely to win. Limbs dropped, spines snapped, jaws broke. Faces behind metal helmets ducked, quavered, crumpled. Sear sliced horizontally, vertically, in and out. She tore armour like it was flesh, and she was but one of many dishing out the punishment. The Crystal Cult were almost entirely unable to lay metal on those from Elsdale. The bodies piled up and the frontline was a climb first before a fight. Few were actually dead yet, and agony covered the battlefield as the dying and maimed begged for their end to come.

Marigold felt heat and strength in his right side as he pushed on.

"Chief," a familiar voice stated by his right, as though they had only seen each other minutes ago. "We're here to bloody avenge you, for fuck's sake."

"Vik! Sorry to disappoint you with my still beating heart. Having fun?" he panted.

"Most certainly am, thought my axe was going to fucking rust before you got yourself lost. Not had a decent scrap in weeks."

"I wasn't fucking lost, Vik!" Marigold barked back. "I was on a fucking job. Still am, if you can't tell."

But on Vik pushed, into the mass of metal and blue, hacking this way and that with joy etched on his face. Arsehole. His large frame was replaced by the stout shoulders of Gunnar, his thick, black ponytail already dripping with blood.

"We still settling Illis, Chief, or 'as this fucked us?"

"Finding the fight tough, Gunnar?"

"Hardly, Chief, I'm using my fingers and a shitting dagger here, and it's mostly my fingers." Gunnar thrust ahead, right through the slit in the helmet of the cultist before them. He left the small blade wedged there as desperate hands grappled at the hilt. He ignored the claymore still strapped behind him and carried on doling out the punishment with his fists.

"Then what do you think?"

"Say we set up camp outside the forest," he panted. "Say we use these capes for a fuckin' tent!"

"Then you'd better gather them up."

Gunnar batted Knife-Eye's hands away and plucked the weapon back for himself. He booted the blinded man to the earth and cut faster than before, clearing a gap as three shrieking cultists crumpled. Marigold's boot slipped in the mess of tangled innards and he was forced to a knee to steady himself. A shadow rose over him.

The shadow gurgled.

Marigold held a deadweight back with his free arm to find a bolt embedded in the soft, fleshy indent of the neck of his would-be assassin. A fine mist of blood spewed from the edge of the wound. A familiar bolt. Marigold pushed himself up to find the source, swinging Sear as he glanced back. A nod came from a dark-haired face between the bare shoulders of old friends.

Ramage.

The cunt was actually alive, and he'd finally killed someone with that fucking crossbow.

A grin and a flash of white teeth, and the woodcutter was lost from view.

Blue surrounded Marigold. Where had he ended up? Shoulders slick with cultist blood saw him sliding between the ranks of slippery armour, over into enemy lines. A blade nicked his shoulder, right over that fucking slice from back in the mountain. Now he was going to have a cross-shaped scar. A cape wrapped itself around his trunk. He wound it up with his free arm and brought a squealing cultist's face below to his belly button. "You considered dropping the capes yet?" he yelled, smashing Sear's hilt down into the centre of the metal helmet. The crushing dent tore the eye slit wide open. The face within couldn't have been older than Pettar. And now it was just as dead as Pettar, too.

The body fell and the battlefield floor rose further.

"To me! To me!" yelled a hoarse and commanding voice.

And just where the fuck was that noise coming from? It was the first order he'd heard from the enemy.

"Men, on me. Now!" the rasping voice was thin, but loud. Important. "Our Lord and my son have both perished at the hands of Elsdale. Retribution will be swift! No mercy for any! Kill them all! All! Death to them all!"

The cult certainly *looked* organised – what, with everyone wearing the same – but so far, they had been about as coordinated as a man after a barrel-full of Elsdale's finest, simply throwing the numbers they had at what they thought would be the weaker side. Well, who was forming up now? Who was actually having to think about employing something along the lines of tactics?

Marigold toppled forwards as the line of the Crystal Cult before him retreated. He anchored himself with Sear plunged deep into a misshapen corpse as the line ahead dissolved.

"To the Captain! To Cecil!" cried a young, high-pitched voice from within the mass retreating from Marigold's side of the fighting line.

Captain Cecil? *The* Cecil.

Marigold paced backwards, watching the point upon which capes were forming. Right back at the treeline by the ragged and grey cliffs of Spitertind. Within the middle stood a man in shining silver chainmail as cultists built a rank behind him. The man wore no blue cape – possibly explaining how he had reached his age – and no helmet. A curved sword gleamed in each hand. From this distance the finer details weren't exactly clear, but this new contender had silver hair as bright as his armour, and a short beard of the same hue framing his angular face. Shorter than his men, very skinny, old, yet exuding a dangerous confidence. Marigold had a bad feeling that this cunt actually knew how to fight, simply by the way he held himself. "All of you!" he bellowed, "On the old fucker, now! If he goes down, they're- FUCK!" Marigold roared, falling onto the bodies below him. Sear slid between bloodied arms. A sharp point of pressure in his back blossomed into a cascade of agony that shot up his spine and around his ribs. Through pain-scrunched eyes he watched his side surge upon Cecil's.

"And just like that the Worm's Will is done!" a vaguely familiar voice whispered from behind.

Marigold sent exploratory fingers to the source of the pain and kept a watering eye on the Elsdale folk and barbarians trampling into battle without him. A handle was sticking out of his lower back. A bone handle, as irrelevant as that was at this point. A stab wound was a stab wound.

"Ah, shit. Shit, shit, shit, shit, SHIT! Why didn't you just die?" the voice became panicked. More metal slid from leather.

Marigold rolled over mangled bodies to face his attacker, shoving the dagger agonisingly deeper in the process. A short, tubby man with a black mop of hair stood gawping, one hand shook around a second knife as the other frantically brushed hair from eyes. "Christian?" Marigold spat. "What the fuck is this?" A mistake? No. This stoneless shit had quoted cult words at him. "You…" Marigold gasped in pain, "you let them know we were coming! That's how Lennan knew of Pettar!"

"Let them know? What, you think I ran up there ahead of you? Have you seen the state of me? No, I don't visit the hallowed ones, I stay in the inn, keep the fire going."

Knife or no knife, Marigold's torso muscles still flexed with all their usual magnificence, and in the blink of an eye a powerful sit-up launched him to his feet. His fingers wrapped around Christian's second knife hand and twisted. He snapped the pathetic wrist that held it as he turned the point on its owner. As the bones of Christian's arm tore through his skin, the blade plunged deep between the bartender's ribs. Barely a sound left the stricken man's lips.

Christian's eyes widened in horror. "Weren't… meant…" he spluttered.

"What? What?! You had that shitting knife ready for me this whole time?"

"Russel…"

"Still angry about that? Well Russel's still dead and you're about to discover what that's like."

"Weren't… meant to…" Christian coughed up a trickle of blood, "get out…"

"And yet we did," Marigold headbutted the fat bastard with a hollow clonk. "You want to kill a man like me, you go for the neck, the heart, fuck, even the stones. Did you even take a look at my back before you stuck your needle in it? Did it look like the kind of back that would work with your idiotic plan? See the wounds that haven't stopped me yet? You've barely pierced the fucking surface!" In the safety of his own mind, Marigold knew the wound was set to be a serious problem but he couldn't be having the weasel's soul leave its body while clinging to even the merest shred of satisfaction.

"The Crystal… will…"

"Oh, fuck off." Marigold threw the gasping weasel to the wet grass. Let the fetid ringpiece live out his final moments with words to say to no-one but himself and the dead. He fingered the edge of the knife hilt again and bit his lip. Could pull it out, could leave it in. He couldn't see it, but right now it was probably plugging some sickening reservoir of blood. Blood he was going to need for the rest of the fight. It wasn't the first time he had been stabbed in the back. Shit, it wasn't even the first time he been stabbed in that exact spot. Probably wouldn't kill him, but it wasn't going to make fighting that bony old bastard in charge of the cultists any easier. Another kill he was going to have to leave to someone else. Again. He could almost hear Greldin's booming laughter behind him, "*Prove yourself as Chief.*"

It had never occurred to him that Christian was an agent of the cult. Then again, he hadn't even known of the Crystal Cult when Christian had laid out who they were. Shithead had seemed so sincere. Perfect prick for the job, then. He collected Sear from the bodies at his feet. "Fuck's sake," he muttered to himself as he stumbled over arms and legs and torsos in the direction of battle. Cries of battle and death washed over him. Men fell from the crush on both sides. A body was thrown up above the scrap. The sky seemed brighter. Fuzzy. No, the man wasn't thrown, there was too much control in the flight. The figure in the air had put himself there and it was exactly where he had meant to go. Twin swords flashed in the sun.

Cecil. Nimble for an old shit.

The warrior turned both swords down as gravity pulled him back. Each sword claimed their own victim. The white hair of the acrobat bobbed up and down, zipped in and out and between men. Around he dashed, slicing throats, piercing eyes, tearing chests. A bare-chested barbarian stumbled backwards out of the crowd. Nils, clutching a gash from stomach to shoulders. Not fatal. That'd match the scar on the bastard's back.

Marigold was close to the fight now. A man and woman ran past him, bounding into the fight with a pitchfork and scythe. Marigold twitched. The next Elsdale man, woman, or child to have a knife for him was getting Sear down their throat. He shook his head a little and his eyesight blurred. Nevertheless, here he was, at the back of the fray.

Time for fire.

Marigold plucked Sear's vial from his belt and dropped it into her hilt, licking his lips and swaying uneasily. With a scraping twist, the viscous fluid cloaked the blade. Fuck, he felt sick. He struck her tip across the chest plate of dead cultist and lit her up with her signature roar.

"Chief!" Sieg's familiar voice floated in from somewhere around him.

"Sieg," Marigold said slowly. He felt worse now than he did when he was pissed.

"Fuck me, Chief, you seen the state of your back?" Sieg was at his side now. "You want out of bein' Chief already, Chief?"

"No! No, of course not. I've felt it, all of it, but I can't do anything about that knife when there's fighting to be had. How bad is it?" Sear's heat was welcome warmth against the chill that gripped his body.

"Dunno how long the blade is, like, but it's leaking something rotten. Here..." Sieg's arm snapped out in a dreamlike haze and wrapped itself about a strobing blue and yellow shape. "Watch where you're waving that flaming sword, Chief." The younger barbarian twisted and yanked. Bone snapped from somewhere in the smear ahead. A cultist's head was ripped clean from its shoulders, spraying the pair with blood while the skull sailed harmlessly overhead. Sieg held the long cut of bloodied blue fabric before his Chief and grinned. "Want me to have it out?"

Marigold blinked cultist blood from his eyes. The whole pissing world was swaying before him. "Aye yeah, go on then." What was the worst that could happen? Sear was getting heavy.

A great build-up of pressure was released, and Marigold almost collapsed right there. Within a heartbeat, Sieg tightened the cape around Marigold's midriff. A new pressure, but a more welcome one. Marigold took deep breaths, fighting off the raging nausea.

"A cape? Told Ramage I'd..." Greldin, he was feeling woozy, "I'd kill him. With a cape on. If he wore a cape."

"Ramage? Anyway, you'll be alright, Chief. You've had worse. The rest of your back looks more savage, if I'm bein' honest, and that's not fucked ya. Y' been fightin' bears again?"

"Aye." Marigold steeled himself and forced his eyes to focus ahead. In through the nose, out through the mouth. The cape tourniquet helped a little, he didn't feel so... *loose*. The numbers on both sides were dwindling, though neither side would accept the loss. Cecil was still there darting about, swinging with wild precision, dropping barbarians and townsfolk with equal ease. Who the fuck was this character? Where had he learned to fight like that when his cultist friends barely knew how to hold a sword? Without realising what he was doing, Sear's blazing tip set the cultists before Marigold alight. Coordination within the battle became every man for himself as the flames leapt from cloak to cloak all while the volatile fluid was flung about in drips and drabs. Sear's fires were almost impossible to extinguish until they decided they wanted to go out, large bodies of water not permitting. The flames grew, caring not for friend or foe. It was difficult to know just who was who, everyone looked to be the same shadowy figure. He was calm though; his men knew when to stand back while Sear was raging. This battle was ending soon.

The gathering began to split. Burning folk frantically tried to douse their flames. Cultists tore hysterically at their ridiculous capes while the blaze ate through them. The clash faltered. People of all sides fled, but it was Marigold's men that had taken to chasing down the escapees as they made for the treeline. Marigold furrowed his brow to focus on Cecil. The swordsman stood a good few paces ahead amidst the remnants of fighters that were still going at it. Now they stood almost face-to-face, Marigold could see that the man was short, even slight. Didn't change the fact that he fought like a demon. Henrik, a fine barbarian of Marigold's age, ran in from the side, sensing an opening. Without even a glance, Cecil stabbed outwards, sliding the tip of his blade through Henrik's mouth and out the neck at the back, metal ground on bone. The warrior crumpled to the ground in silence as the weapon was withdrawn.

"Leader of this group of savages, are you?" the ancient man rasped at Marigold, pacing ever closer. A gleam like that of a rabid dog lit his eyes.

"Apparently so," panted Marigold, spitting bile to the earth. "You're Cecil, right?" One of two Cecils thanks to his rolling eyes.

"Aye, and you're wounded. Not going to last long."

"I'll last longer than Russel or your worm did."

"It was you?"

"Russel? Oh, everyone had a hand in that," he lied, "nobody could get enough of sliding their knives in and out. Steak knives, you know? Really put the '*cut*' in cutlery."

Cecil charged, fury raging in his sunken eyes. He struck like a viper. Marigold still had the wherewithal to block the twin blades as they clanged around him, but he needed the strength of both arms to hold Sear now. Between the flames and the metal clashing, the old man's face darted in and out, lit up hideously. Barely more than a skull, pale skin clung to the sharp angles of bone. Sunken cheeks and hollow temples were devoid of spare flesh. His sparse, white beard barely had anything to cling to. Liver spots peppered the swordsman's tight forehead until it reached the thin and brittle white hair on top. A ring on a chain, a gold band, glinted from his neck. Must have outlived his woman, shit, the man must have been a hundred years old. Brown teeth clenched tightly behind thin, pink lips. Spittle flicked out between the gaps. Grunts and groans suggested that while Cecil was an excellent fighter, age still called the shots where exertion was concerned. From Marigold's point of view, he was doing all he could to stop another cut of metal entering the more important areas of his flesh. He hadn't been on this much of a back foot since taking on a company of roughskins alone as a lad.

And then there it was. The slip.

The tip of one of Cecil's blades pierced the middle Marigold's thigh. Another fine scar to add to the collection if it ever got the chance to heal.

It was a wound that he would normally ride out with ease, but with the pain in his back and the haze in his head, this new hole to lose blood from quickly took its toll. As the second sword came down for the Chief's neck, Marigold threw a last burst of strength into hurling Sear up.

A hiss, a slice, a crackle.

He'd intended to stop the sword where it was, but the happier result saw Cecil's left arm pirouette through the air, still clutching its deadly weapon. Pity he'd also cauterised the wound for the cunt.

Cecil made no sound, even with his mortal injury; it wouldn't have been a surprise to hear that his nerves had died off long ago. But instead of staggering in horror at the loss of the limb, he sprung up, out of the reach of Sear's fiery bite and into the air. It was as though the man had wings, having the time while airborne to punt Marigold in the side of the face with each metal-booted foot. The battered barbarian hit the grass black-eye-first, the blood-tipped blades tickling his face and eyes. Sear burned impotently away at the earth by his side. A cooling patch of snow soothed his pierced thigh.

Here was the end.

No more Elvi. No more battles to be won. No more adventures to be had.

At least that bony prick was going to follow shortly after. If he didn't just drop dead then one of his men would see to putting that rat out of its misery and that man or woman would end up as the next chief.

Metal rung on metal. Bone crunched.

Marigold certainly didn't feel anything. Was that really how death was?

"You'll take that for everything you've done, y'old cunt, so you will!"

Marigold began laughing gently into the sodden grass, partly in despair. The laugh became a cough, became spasms of pain. With a light thud, Cecil's dead-eyed face came to rest in the flattened grass by Marigold, staring directly at him as the remnants of life faded. The look of surprise on him was most satisfying.

"You've betrayed a god. You've killed my..." And Cecil was gone. That part was not quite as satisfying.

A momentary silence fell on the open land around Elsdale. Gasps and murmurs from the living cultists broke it, quickly drowned out by metal-booted feet fleeing the scene, and leather-booted feet chasing them down.

With an effort that had to rank high among his greatest feats of strength, Marigold pushed himself up onto his arse. He crossed his legs, chiefly to steady himself. Cecil wasn't getting up. Cecil wasn't going to sit on *his* arse. Ramage stood close, hands held defiantly on his hips, crossbow on his back. At least he had secured some clothing before joining the fight. His axe – a great, two-handed bastard that he must have picked up on his return to Elsdale – was deeply buried within Cecil's back. So fierce had the blow been that it had simply pushed Cecil's shining chainmail into the chasm it had created. There wasn't much blood, just a glistening around the edges of the wound. Old bastard probably had shit circulation at that age anyway, or else had nothing more than dust in his veins. Cecil's remaining hand was propped up, still gripping the sword that had poked point first into the earth as he fell.

"Fine work, Ramage. I knew you were alright," Marigold said, woozily. He looked at the hole in his thigh. Narrow, but deep. Perhaps it would sometimes be a good idea to don a bit of armour.

"Up you get, Chief," Vik's voice boomed.

The sun, directly overhead, dazzled Marigold as he looked up to the arms of Vik and Dolph. He felt like he floated up. The hum of battle was dying down. A call here and there directed the remnants, a terrified scream every now and then hailed the close of the fight. Marigold felt arms about shoulders. He shook them free.

"Lads, lads, it's alright, I can walk. Can't leave Sear down there, can I?" His voice was soft, quiet. Was he going to be sick or had he been sick?

"She ain't down there, I got her right here, Chief," Dolph said.

"Pass... her here, then," Marigold wobbled.

"You alright, Chief?" Many voices asked that. Where were they all?

Marigold looked at his empty palm. Sear had just been placed there. Where was she again? There was an odd aura around his fingers. Everything became very bright and hazy, very quickly.

There was the grass on his cheek again.

It certainly wasn't bright now. There was barely any light at all. Marigold strained his eyes as he tried to pierce the depths of the dark abyss above him.

What? By fucking Greldin, either he was dead or he'd dreamt that entire-

"Back among the living, are we?" Marigold's favourite voice slipped through the gloom.

"Elvi?" Marigold jerked up, immediately wincing at the pain in his back. He was low to the ground. But that was her alright, starting to kneel down by the cot in which he lay. He focused on the little scar that drew up the side of her lips. Once he had that clear, he met the green jewels that were her eyes. She looked happy to see him. Shit. Marigold chewed his lip like a boy might. He was about to shatter that warm happiness. "Elvi, I've bad news, I... I..."

"I know. Magnus told me as soon as he found me," she said quietly. "It sounds as though he finally grew up." There were no sobs, but Marigold watched her head drop. She sniffed loudly but without tears and stared over Marigold's head.

"I couldn't stop it. Elvi, I mean, it was my idea to go, to bring him along, we shouldn't have-"

A burst of light split the room. A flimsy door rattled against a wooden wall as it was kicked open. Marigold shielded his eyes and squinted between his fingers. A dark frame silhouetted the doorway.

"You up yet, Chief, you lazy cunt?" the shadow said.

"Magnus? Fuck off, have you seen the state of me?" He was still leader of the clan though, it seemed.

"Aye, Chief. New scars. Good fight though, eh?" Magnus boomed. "Nothing like bloodied knuckles to round off a job." He cracked them to prove a point. "Smashed a good few jaws in that scrap, felt good. You get many yourself, Chief?"

"One or two. That fucking bartender was one of them. Christian, did you hear? Cultist bastard all along and he stabbed me in the back." Marigold shifted on the downy base beneath his arse, putting himself into a position that didn't remind him of the wound. It felt remarkably better though.

"They know alright, these Elsdale folk that are left threw his corpse on the pyre with the rest of the cult. Ties've been cut clean, an' his booze is up for grabs as well." Magnus illustrated the fact with a swig from an almost empty bottle that he produced from his hip. "They didn't have any idea, but now they're all murmuring about whether or not he had anything to do with the disappearance of the owner of the other inn the town had. Mary, or summats. Went missing a while back apparently, but nobody saw the cult take her. Since then, everyone ended up together in Christian's place. Easy for the blue-cloaks to find them when they were all rounded up in one place."

"Stoneless bastard. What about Haggar, he with Greldin or us?"

"Ha! With us, Chief, Greldin didn't want him," Magnus began to chuckle. "Got smashed over the head at the start of the fight and was out cold for the rest of it. Didn't even get trampled. He's out there right now trying to tell everyone how he lost his tongue. Dumb prick hasn't realised he can't do that yet, but maybe it'll save him some embarrassment in the long run. Everyone'll probably think he lost it in the mountain."

"How did he lose his tongue?" Elvi asked.

"Thought he could be the showman," Marigold explained. "Fire and drink were the setpieces and then it all went a bit south."

"Was it for a couple of girls?" she asked.

"Four of 'em."

An impressed smirk cracked Elvi's face.

"Anyway, Chief," Magnus continued, "I brought you some new skins." He dumped them on the end of the low bed. "Something a bit warmer for you while you recover and they'll hide some of the bandages: gotta look invincible to the crew, right? Besides, there's a nip on the winds even if the ground snow's mostly gone, and we don't want you coming down with 'owt on top of healing, do we? If you're feeling up to it, come outside and find Ramage. Fucker killed Cecil, didn't he? He's become something of the leader of this little place on the back of that. I mean, there's only a handful of the bastards left, but it's pretty good for him, eh?"

"It's not bad," Marigold agreed. "I'll be out later on, just give me a moment to wipe the cobwebs away, my head still feels like it's cracked." Marigold looked at the cup on the floor by his bed suspiciously. "You've not been watering me with ale, have you?" He asked Magnus and Elvi.

"No, my love, you just lost a lot of blood. A lot."

Marigold noted Magnus's eyebrows raise and smiled warmly. Well, that was one way to make it official, if a little unexpected given how well he had fucked everything up.

"I'll leave you to it, Chief. Me and the lads are putting up some shacks for those what're left. Plenty o'trees around, but only a few houses and little sheds like this left unburned. Suggested using the bones o' the cultists as a frame, but they weren't into that, for some reason."

And with that, Magnus left the impromptu house of healing.

What to say? It was just the two of them again. If he was being honest with himself, he didn't feel up to pulling her on top of him right now. He *really* had to be in a bad way to feel like that. The wounds on his arms and legs and shoulders were bandaged. He couldn't see how bad they were, but he seemed to be more bandage than man right now. Shit. Don't let the silence ruin it. "I'll bring him back," he blurted out. What the fuck? Why was he taking the conversation back to grief? What part of him thought that was a good idea?

"I'll come with you, we'll bring him back together." Elvi squeezed Marigold's hand.

Did Greldin owe him a favour or something? Perhaps his subconscious really did know best, it had kept him alive in that river, after all.

Marigold lay back on the bed and closed his eyes. He felt the warmth of Elvi as she shuffled onto the narrow frame and lay down next to him. Fuck the pain in his leg as she leaned on it; she could lean on it all she wanted. This was what he had wanted for a long time.

The sun had long set when Marigold finally emerged from the hut with Elvi. Rudimentary torches were stuck into the mud here and there, and dotted in a rough circle around the remaining housing of Elsdale. Marigold noted the tell-tale blue of the Crystal Cult's capes burning as fuel atop each of them. There were several new buildings filling the gaps where wide streets had once been, and plenty of charred piles of wood from demolished housing that had fallen to the cult's attack. One of those piles had been Christian's inn. Whether that was burned before or after his betrayal was uncovered, Marigold didn't follow up on.

Marigold and Elvi wandered around the new housing in the direction of a pale smoke that rose up into the clear night sky. Elsdaler and barbarian alike were sat on flat cuts of log, eating and drinking, and generally carrying on in good spirits. The number of Elsdale folk left was around half what Marigold had noted before they had set off for the mountain. Damn shame. Marigold sniffed as he sat down between Nils and Haggar, catching the unmistakeable smell of charred flesh as he dropped – when you slew men regularly with a burning blade, it was an aroma you quickly became familiar with. A large pile, almost by the treeline, looked to the be the source. There was a decent group of his clan at the fire, but only a fraction of the forces he had left behind on his trip into Elsdale. Bad news or a small rescue party. Ramage was sat on the far side of the fire, quietly talking with none other than Nina. Marigold was pleased to see that she had made it out, especially since rescuing her had very nearly resulted in his death. To his right, Haggar had one of the girls from that first night in the inn on his knee. Fucking typical. Vik and Dolph were sat partway around the circle, chewing on some meat and showing off their boot daggers to a group of interested Elsdale folk. Around the fire, Nils, Einer, and Britt sat bandaged almost as heavily as Marigold. Haggar had barely a scratch on him save for a small welt on his temple. Chatter was a dull murmur, but everyone was getting along.

"Made it out then, Chief," Magnus winked.

"Yup. Had a fine sleep." And he had, he'd fallen asleep almost immediately, no funny business. "You've made great bloody progress, eh?" He said, nodding in turn at the new buildings on show. "How'd you knock them up so quick?"

"You fucking idiot, Chief," Magnus laughed.

Haggar slapped Marigold across the back, recoiling immediately upon realising what he had hit. He held his palms up and opened his empty mouth in apology.

"What? Why'm I a fucking idiot?" Marigold winced.

"It's been four pissing days, Chief," Sieg broke in. "You've been sleeping it off while the rest of us have been grafting to get these fine folks back up a standard of living they can abide by."

"Ah…" he croaked pathetically. Maybe he really hadn't had worse before. As far as he knew, he'd never been out for over a day either. Even after one of Haggar's piss-ups. That tubby fucker with the knife had nearly done him in, then. After all he had been through in his lifetime.

"Here, have this," Dolph reached for a skewer over the fire and passed a chunk of dripping meat to Marigold. "Goat, not cultist," he laughed. "Ale in the barrel, too. Might have to dunk your head though, think we're out of cups."

"We had caught some fish," Ramage broke in from across the fire, "but they all seem to be off an account of the worm guts that are flowing out of the mountain, so they are. It'll be goat and veg for a while, I think."

"Aye, whole river fucking stinks," Vik said grumpily. Well, Vik liked a fish.

Nina and Ramage got up from their seats and wandered over to Marigold. Elvi shuffled over and began talking with Nils. Something about the number of buildings that were still to come.

"Marigold," Ramage greeted as he sat directly on the grass before him, grinning widely. "You've saved our town, so you have. Well, village, I suppose now."

"You made the killing blow, Ramage, more than once," Marigold said, a little regretfully now that it was out in the open. "And really, Ramage, I am sorry about the losses you've all been dealt. Elsdale'll be a town again soon."

"It's a blow, so it is, but each and everyone one of these folks who died, did so knowing they were dying for change instead of dying for nothing. Truth be told, they're having a hard time coming to terms with what was actually going on in there, so they are." He slowly gazed back upon the mountain. "If it weren't for you, we'd all have been fed to that worm eventually, so we would."

"And I have some thanks to give too, now that we're giving it," Nina chimed in. "Not only did you save my life, Marigold, you also managed to bring down the rakeworm and have all of you make it out ali-" She paused and blinked in the direction of Elvi. "A-All Sistren that have felled a worm have died with the worm according to our records. I know it will be difficult, and I've no doubt we'll lose more trying, but perhaps now, not every assassination attempt will also double as a suicide mission."

"Well, you know, it wasn't fucking easy!" Marigold said, pulling at the hem of his furs with a finger as he remembered the suffocating heat of the worm's throat. "I mean, I think we only survived because Lennan had us chained together. Pit-spawned worm couldn't swallow us like that. But I'll tell you this, if you're planning on finding another of these worm cunts, you make sure you stay out of the stomach while the poison takes hold. That was our escape. That poison works quickly, and once it does, the whole worm seems to relax. Then you can cut it, or it'll split itself open as it thrashes about." He didn't want to add that dumb luck seemed to play a rather large part in it.

"I am going to try again," Nina declared. "Before I was captured, there was still a worm north of Rumiruna, you know the place?"

"Aye. Big city, four layers, three towers, two kings, and one huge pain in my stones whenever I've needed to go there. Yes, I know it," said Marigold, begrudgingly remembering the last time he had been there and the miles long chase that had followed after lopping off a thief's head in The Cobbled Mare.

"Well, I've had less trouble there. The rakeworm though, it might still be growing further north. Even without it, I have business in the city that I'd really like to see to," she said. "If she'll still have me," she added quietly.

Marigold gave himself a small nod for just *knowing* that Haggar wasn't her type.

"You're leaving soon, so you are?" Ramage asked, clearly the first he had heard of this.

"Tomorrow, all being well."

"We'll get what we can readied for you, though you'll have to walk, I'm afraid, so you will. We've no carts or the like around."

"Nah." Marigold shook his head. "You can take one of our rukhs, looks like we've a couple spare now. One of the boys'll get her ready. But Nina, don't let this trying again be the end of you," Marigold warned. "I don't doubt your intentions, but we won't be there to rescue you next time. Oh, I'm… er, I'm talking about the rakeworm, not the rukh."

"I'm well aware, Marigold. Besides, I think Lennan was an odd one. I'm sure any other High Priest would have had me killed there and then if they found me out."

"Reassuring," Marigold deadpanned.

"Very," Nina said with a smile. She got up and wandered around the fire to Magnus.

"So, you're Chief now, Ramage," Marigold asked, genuinely curious.

"Chief's a bit strong, don't you think? I'm nothing compared to yourself, so I'm not. But, I went up there with you, so I did, and I came back down. Best decision I ever made, looking back. We don't really have a leader, but it seems me fellows have a newfound respect for me." Ramage lowered his voice and leaned in. "Assuming you never tell them about all the times I went and fucked up in there."

"Secret's safe with me, Ramage. It's safe with Haggar, too. Would you like me to cut Magnus's tongue out as well so that he doesn't go blabbing?"

Ramage laughed uneasily and Marigold knuckled him in the shoulder. He'd had his misgivings about the woodcutter, and with plenty of good reasons. But, the man wasn't a born warrior and he had still made it out of this mess. He was a stout-hearted coward trying to make the best of the shitty situation that his weak god, Fyr, had dealt him. With all things said and done, Ramage had done well, and Greldin would be keeping an eye on him now. That was about as positive a thing as could be said for a man that previously had the certain doom of fizzing away in a worm's stomach hanging over him.

"Once these buildings are up, we'll leave you in peace," Marigold told Ramage. "I doubt we'll be far, but we like to move a bit every now and then, go where the herds go, move on when we exhaust the veins in the hills."

"Ramage, sir," a voice called from over the side of the fire.

"Off you go, sir, looks like you've business to attend to now. Good luck!"

Marigold sat staring at the fire, not alone, but with the backs of friends and Elsdale folk to him. The fire crackled and spat. The meat on those remaining skewers was surely fucked by now. Charred to waste. Beyond the pointed flames, Mt. Spitertind loomed over Elsdale. An obelisk in the night sky, looking just the same now as she had before any of this went down. Rakeworms were not common knowledge for the world, at least as far as Marigold knew. Perhaps Elsdale was among the first to escape complete annihilation at the maw of the beast and the hands of the cult. Perhaps warnings might now filter out, now the folk of Elsdale were free to come and go as they pleased. Maybe the world might yet know of rakeworms. All Marigold knew was that he was staying in Illis, though he would aim for as far from Spitertind as that would allow. Maybe wrangle some goats, get a farm going. This settling lark looked like it could be good for a time. Quite how he had made it from the tavern, up to the top of the mountain, and back out again – and on the winning side of the completely unforeseen battle – *and yet still somehow remain the head of the clan* baffled him. He couldn't even count the mistakes he had made on both hands, and that wasn't because two of his fingers appeared to be broken. They still wanted him, it seemed. Elvi still wanted him. Was he doing this leading thing right? Magnus and Haggar were happy. Ramage was now the head of Elsdale. Russel, Lennan, Cecil, and their vile rakeworm all lay dead. Those victories had come from decisions made by him, even if the results hadn't been enacted by him. Perhaps the Chief didn't have to do it all. Perhaps the Chief only had to facilitate. It wasn't like the role came with any instructions, so perhaps it was alright if he just made it up as he went along. Still, he was never going to forget that his decisions had also left Pettar dead.

A weight around his shoulders increased.

Not a cold weight.

"So. Who's this Nina, hey?" Elvi mocked, elbowing Marigold gently in the ribs as she sat back by his side.

THE TALE RETOLD

In the quiet and desolate town of Elsdale,
Marigold drank at the inn with his friends.
The land of Illis was a land he quite liked,
Fancied settling within to his end.

But good times were doused, the drinks interrupted,
A man from a cult in the mountain.
Demanded a sacrifice to follow him up,
His days were numbered, and Marigold was counting.

The death of the cultist was not taken well,
And Elsdale feared swift retribution.
But Marigold already wanted these lands,
And suggested a means of solution.

The Crystal Cult hid themselves high up top,
Of Mount Spitertind, highest peak in the country.
A quest began through ice, rock, and snow,
Marigold hoped to dispatch them abruptly.

A church at the top was riddled with fools,
Unprepared for the wrath of the men,
One by one their forces fell dead,
But of the cult this was far from the end.

The church was a front, a statue of sorts,
The mere tip of the iceberg below.
Marigold's group climbed down many rough-carven steps,
And to their surprise found the mountain hollow.

But lit was the path that the men now trod,
Fluorescent with Cerulean Hair.
A fungus that clung to the high cavern walls.
And revealed the rest of the lair.

A great tower pulsed in the depths of the pit,
Glowing and beating, alive!
"Quite the wizard we've found," Marigold cried,
And in killing them a barbarian thrived.

A battle broke out, their location revealed,
The men fought doubly hard for their hide.
The cultists were slain, the path opened up,
But of Marigold's men, one had died.

Pettar was young, had not chanced yet to learn,
That teamwork trumps singular pride.
He slew his mark but was knocked from his feet,
With a tick-beast affixed to his side.

The journey had soured, was meant to be easy,
None considered the loss of a life.
More determined than ever, Marigold delved deeper down,
The wizard's head would relieve him his strife.

But down in the base, on the sand of the pit,
The tower was not what it seemed.
No way in or up or out could be found,
Could the mission now not be redeemed?

Marigold's men were caught out by the gathering cult,
Their full force surrounded his four.

The High Priest, Lennan, revealed his face,
Down here, their rules were law.

The Roof was unleashed, a mountain of flesh,
A man, they claimed him to be.
It felled the barbarian and all of his men,
Their bodies no more than debris.

Marigold and his men were led to a cell,
Locked up there and then forced to wait.
The mood of group grew sombre and dark,
With no escape to be found from their fate.

A woman named Nina they met in the cells,
A prisoner, she had dwelt there for years.
She regaled our men with the answers they needed,
Though did nothing to dampen their fears.

The tower was not the abode of a wizard,
Nor was it even a tower.
The shape was a shell, a cocoon, a layer,
For the rakeworm, the cult's source of power.

As Lennan and company arrived for the men,
Nina snuck Marigold a small poison pouch.
To be used only once, when the time was just right,
Marigold assured her that he'd be no slouch.

Chained and bound, the barbarians were led,
Into the depths of the cavern.
Below the tower. The cocoon! The power!
How they wished that they'd not left that tavern.

The maw of the rakeworm howled above,

Hissed and spit and gagged.
The first of our men was unchained and stripped down,
Beneath the mouth of the beast he was dragged.

Marigold screamed that enough was enough,
And despite their situation they fought.
The Roof battled back, he gave it his all,
But in the end, only his death was wrought.

Still chained together, Marigold suggested,
That they rescue their sadly lost number.
Grabbing cult sword and poison they all stood below,
A throat they might over-encumber.

The inside was hot and dark and airless,
To their doom they were inexorably sucked.
Marigold held the pouch between in his cheeks,
Must act fast, before they were all fucked.

They rescued their friend from the lip of stomach,
Acid dripped like unsavoury soup.
Up went the pouch, the poison, the solution,
And to luck tightly clung the whole group.

The worm writhed in agony, the worm shook with death,
And tore itself from its cocoon.
It thrashed around, gashing open its guts,
Granting the men their much-needed boon.

Short-lived were the good times for around the group's
feet,
The cavern had started to flood.
The men ran fast, waded through the vile mess,
To the cell that still held friendly blood.

Nina was freed and the group made their dash,
But the route they came in through had gone.
The only way out lay in rivers below,
Time to run, before routes numbered none!

Thrown and smashed, into rocks they were flung,
Sailed right out of the cave into freedom.
Marigold awoke still submerged in the deep, frozen flood,
And alone he found himself bleeding.

Dazed and confused, and unsure of his friends,
He caught on the wind sounds of battle.
He picked himself up and entered the forest,
This quest had become quite the hassle.

Elsdalers were fighting, the cult had arrived,
Vengeance for the death of their worm!
The fighting looked grim, the conclusion foregone,
But a barbarian detachment stood firm.

Arms and legs and heads and hands,
Littered the fresh-bloodied grass.
The scrapping was fierce, brutal, depraved,
The cultists were dying en masse.

But the Crystal Cult had an ace up its sleeve,
A wizened old fighter named Cecil.
Like a demon he sprung, slashing and piercing,
His delight in the violence quite gleeful.

Marigold readied himself for the fight,
Drew closer and readied old Sear.
But a stab from behind ruined all of his plans,

A knife from a man thought sincere.

Wounded and stumbling and trying to think,
The traitor was slain where he stood.
Marigold staggered, back into the fight,
The result was not going to be good.

Cecil thought fast, Cecil fought hard,
Our barbarian now on the back foot.
But a chance stroke of luck sliced the cult leader's arm,
Sear charred the stump to soot.

A friend from behind dealt the blow that would kill,
An axe buried deep in the spine.
The cult were undone, dying or fled,
Mount Spitertind again stood benign.

The victory was hollow and lacking in grace,
The quest to impress unfulfilled.
The cult might have gone, fled to the hills,
Still Marigold's young friend lay killed.

But Chief he remained, despite his missteps,
The clan still saw him as lord.
Sear in his hand and Elvi at his side,
His faith in himself was restored.

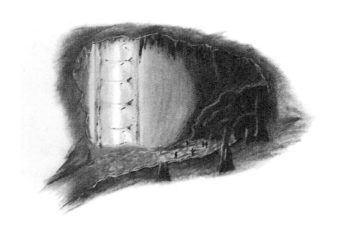

Printed in Great Britain
by Amazon